A Dream

Too Far

Seymour and Chris
Summer Lake Silver Book Two

By SJ McCoy

A Sweet n Steamy Romance

Published by Xenion, Inc

Copyright © 2019 SJ McCoy

Published by Xenion, Inc.
First paperback edition 2019
www.sjmccoy.com

This book is a work of fiction. Names, characters, places, and events
are figments of the author's imagination, fictitious, or are used
fictitiously. Any resemblance to actual events, locales or persons
living or dead is coincidental.

Cover Design by Dana Lamothe of Designs by Dana
Editor: Mitzi Pummer Carroll
Proofreaders: Aileen Blomberg, Marisa Nichols, Traci Atkinson,
Jennifer Solymosi.

ISBN: 978-1-946220-57-8

Dedication

This one's for you, Chris—finally.

Thank you being such a good friend to me over these last few years – and thank you for the influence you've had on the lives of our Summer Lake family.

You've been Jack and Dan's mum in my mind for a long time now. I kept promising you a story of your own and here it is. I hope you'll love Seymour. I do!

My only regret with this one is that the character of Jack and Dan's mum already had a difficult past when I gave her your name.

Chapter One

"Sorry I'm late," said Marianne as she came rushing toward the bar where Chris was sitting.

Chris smiled as her sister took a seat beside her. "There's no need to apologize. I wouldn't expect anything else."

Marianne shrugged. "We are what we are. You're always early. I'm always late. If we don't know each other well enough by now…"

"Not so long ago I would've said that I know you better than anyone else on earth and I love you just the way you are. Now, I'd hazard a guess that Clay knows you even better than I do, and we all know he loves you just the way you are, too. Where is he? I thought he might come with you."

Chris loved the way her sister smiled at the mention of her fiancé's name. "He sends his best and said to say he'll see you at the weekend. He has work he wanted to catch up on, and besides, I wanted you all to myself."

"Aww, you know I don't mind when he joins us. I think the world of him. I hope he doesn't think he wouldn't be welcome. I know the two of you seem to do everything together these days."

"No! He knows he's welcome. In fact, if it were down to him, he would have joined us." Marianne smiled. "If you must know, I told him I wanted you all to myself."

Chris laughed. "Let me guess, the novelty of spending every waking moment with him is wearing off?"

"Not at all!" Marianne shook her head emphatically. "I thought it might have by now, but it really hasn't. We get along so well, it's so easy. It's just wonderful, Chris!"

"Aww." Chris reached across and squeezed her sister's arm. "I'm so happy for you and for him. You two are just perfect together. So, tell me, how was Nashville?"

"It was wonderful. I'm starting to really feel at home there. Shawnee is wonderful. She sends her regards and asks when you're going to come visit her, and everyone else is so friendly and welcoming, too. I thought I'd struck it lucky when I moved here. This is such a wonderful place filled with such lovely people. It's hard to believe that now I have a second place and a second group of people that are just as welcoming."

Chris nodded. "We sure landed on our feet here. I'm so pleased that the kids found this place and moved here and I'm even happier that they wanted us to join them. I'm happy here. It's a good place. Of course," she laughed, "I'd be even happier if I could follow in your footsteps and meet an amazing guy like Clay."

Marianne made a face. "Sometimes, I feel bad that I—"

Chris wagged a finger at her. "Don't you dare go saying that you feel bad about any of the wonderful things that are going on in your life. Especially, not if you were about to say what I think you were, that you feel bad that you found love and I haven't."

Marianne shrugged. "I can't help it. Don't get me wrong, I'm so grateful for Clay. It's just that I want the same for you."

It was Chris's turn to shrug. "And don't you get me wrong I'm not sure I'd even want it; I'm fine just the way I am, but I'm so happy for you."

"Hey, Marianne. What can I get you?" Kenzie, the bartender, smiled at them. "If you're having lunch, you can choose any table you like, and I'll bring your drinks and menus over."

Chris led Marianne over to one of the raised booths and took a seat.

Marianne chuckled as she sat down opposite her. "It's a good thing that we're so different in so many respects."

Chris smiled. She knew exactly what she meant. While Marianne preferred to turn her back on the restaurant and focus in on the conversation they were having, Chris preferred to sit where she could keep an eye on the whole place. She was just as focused on the conversation with her sister, but she liked to know what was going on around them.

"We complement each other well."

"So," said Marianne, "tell me what's been going on while I've been away."

"You know me; I've been a busy bee. I seem to be spending most of my time at the women's center. Except, of course, when I'm watching little Isabel for Jack and Emma. Oh, and last week, I was helping Scott with a project for school."

Marianne gave her a puzzled look. "Forgive me, but Scott is so smart, I have to ask what you were helping him with."

Chris had to laugh. "That's what I thought when he first asked me to help him. I had no clue what I would be able to do that he couldn't figure out for himself. It turns out that he needed to interview old people for some project on the aging population."

Marianne's hand came up to cover her mouth, but it couldn't contain her laughter.

Chris gave her a rueful smile. "It's a good thing that I can see the funny side."

"It is funny, but it's not as though you're old enough to really be his grandma."

Chris scowled. "As far as I'm concerned, I really am his grandma."

"Yes, but you know what I mean. I only meant age-wise."

"Yeah, sorry, I didn't mean to jump down your throat. I just get so defensive about him. I love him to little pieces, and come on, he couldn't be more like Dan's son if he were Dan's son."

"That's true." Marianne frowned and looked at the wall above Chris's shoulder.

"What's up? Am I boring you? You just drifted away on me."

Marianne gave her a guilty smile. "I think I have to let you in on a secret."

"Oh yeah, what's that?"

"You think that when we sit here, I'm oblivious to everything else that's going on. I'm not. Those pictures on the wall behind you are mirrored and every now and then I take a peek." She gave Chris a guilty smile.

Chris had to laugh. "You sneaky little … And what did you see in the mirror that had you looking so concerned?" Chris scanned the restaurant but didn't see anything out of the ordinary.

"Well, I thought I saw Chance."

"That's right, Missy mentioned that he and Hope might be visiting sometime soon." She couldn't figure out the weird smile on Marianne's face. "What are you looking like that for?"

"Did Missy say who would be coming with him?"

"Hope, of course, why? Who else …? Oh!" Chris stopped scanning the room and dropped her eyes. "Is he here? Did you see him?"

Marianne laughed. "Yes, I did. I thought you'd be thrilled that he's here. But, look at you! What's up? You can't tell me you don't want him to notice you? You've talked about him for the last couple of years. And I know you've been hoping he would come up here ever since that night in LA."

"Of course, I want him to notice me. Just not right now. Look at me! I'm a mess!"

Marianne laughed again. "You don't have it in you to be a mess. You're always so well put together. And you're beautiful. I should turn around and wave at Chance if you're not going to."

"No! Don't you dare!"

"Why not? Don't you at least want to find out how long he's going to be here?"

"Of course, I do. But I can ask Missy."

Marianne started to turn around, but Chris hissed at her. "Don't you dare!"

It was too late. Chance and Hope were standing at the bar, and Seymour was standing with them. Chris's heart fluttered in her chest at the sight of him; he was just as handsome as she remembered. Well, it wasn't as though she hadn't seen him in the last couple of years; he showed up on TV every couple of months or so. Usually, though, that meant he was dressed in a business suit and was talking about stocks and shares and investments—about his world, a world she knew next to nothing about.

There was no mistaking that the man standing at the bar was the same man, but he looked so very different. If it were possible, he might be even more attractive, dressed casually as he was in jeans and a light blue sweater.

She watched as he leaned over the bar to tell Kenzie what he wanted to drink. She smiled to herself wondering if it would be the same bourbon he'd been drinking that night they met in LA. That seemed so long ago now.

As if he felt her gaze on him, he looked up, directly at her. For a moment, her heart seemed to stop beating. Then he smiled, and it started again with a thud, feeling as though it wanted to beat out of her chest.

She smiled back, and in that moment, it felt as though the distance between them and everything around them melted away. It felt just like it had that night when they talked. They'd been in a busy nightclub, but it felt as though they were all alone in the world.

"I guess you won't need to ask Missy now."

Marianne's voice got through to her but couldn't break the moment. Chris still couldn't tear her eyes away from Seymour's.

"Are we going down there? Or ... Never mind. I think it's time for me to go and powder my nose."

Chris smiled as she sensed Marianne getting up from the table. She couldn't say she saw her go because her gaze was fixed on Seymour, who was now making his way across the restaurant toward their table.

Her mind raced with a dozen thoughts. Her practical voice was telling her to be calm. But most of the other thoughts were chattering in excitement.

When he was just a few feet away, he smiled, and she smiled back.

"Chris! It's great to see you."

She got to her feet, not knowing if she planned to shake his hand or quite what she was going to do. "It's wonderful to see you too. I'm glad you finally made it up here."

She felt foolish when his smile faded. She shouldn't have said that. He'd told her that he would come to Summer Lake, but that had been part of a bigger conversation, a conversation about the possibility of the two of them getting to know each other better.

"I mean ... I know Chance and Hope have been wanting to get you out here. You work so hard. That's all I mean."

His smile was back. It softened his features. He was one of those men who looked kind of imposing, if not intimidating. But when he smiled ...

"Is that really all you meant?" He held her gaze for a long moment, and there was no way she could lie to him.

She shrugged and gave him a rueful smile. "No, it just seemed like the more socially acceptable thing to say."

He laughed, a low deep rumble that made Chance and Hope turned to look in their direction. "That's more like it. That's the Chris I thought you were."

She felt foolish. She held out her hand to shake with him, not knowing what else to do or say. "Either way, I'm glad you're here."

"So am I." Instead of shaking with her, he held his arms out just a little way to his sides. "I know I'm supposed to be the formal one around here, but is there any chance I could get a hug?"

The way her heart was hammering in her chest, she knew he must be able to feel it as she all too briefly leaned against him. His arms closed around her in what must have looked like nothing more than a friendly greeting, but just for a moment, he tightened his arms holding her close, and she squeezed him back. It felt like they had an entire conversation in that one brief embrace.

She stepped back and smiled at him. "How long are you here for?"

He laughed again. "I don't have a fixed plan. The kids want me to stay until next weekend. Maybe, now, I will."

Chris heard herself sucking in a deep breath. He couldn't mean that the way it sounded; he couldn't mean that seeing her might be enough to affect his plans.

He was holding her gaze. "I know it's been a long time, but I said that when I came up here, I might have reached a point where I'd be able to ask you out to dinner."

She nodded, not knowing if he was actually asking or just reminding her of their conversation.

He smiled, and she loved the way the lines creased around his eyes. "If I were to ask, would you say yes?"

"I would."

"May I have your number?" He pulled his phone out of his pocket and looked at her expectantly.

She watched him type in her number as she told it to him.

"Okay." He closed his phone and looked up at her. The imposing businessman was nowhere to be seen. The look in his eyes was raw, uncertain, she almost wanted to hug him again to reassure him, though of what she didn't know. "I'll give you a call tomorrow."

"I'll look forward to it." She leaned toward him and for an all too brief moment, he placed his hands on her hips and bent his head to drop a kiss on her cheek.

"I'm sorry it's taken me so long," he said before turning and walking away.

Her heart raced as she watched him go. Had he really just said that? Or was it just her imagination, wishful thinking on her part?

His daughter, Hope, caught her eye and gave her an encouraging smile.

~ ~ ~

Seymour shoved his hands in his pockets as he walked back across the restaurant to Hope and Chance. Well, he'd done it. Part of him wished he had more time to prepare. He'd thought that he would look her up while he was here, not that he'd run into her the moment he arrived. But still, part of him was glad that it had worked out this way. This way, he didn't have time to talk himself out of it yet again. He'd been doing that for such a long time now.

Hope reached out and squeezed his arm when he reached her. "Are you okay, Dad?"

He gave her what he hoped was a reassuring smile and nodded. "I am."

"What did you say? Did you ask her out to dinner?"

Seymour had to smile at the way Chance frowned at Hope. He didn't say a word; Seymour doubted that he ever had or would reprimand her. He didn't need to. The two of them had such an understanding, Hope immediately knew what he meant.

She came and slid her arm around Seymour's waist. "I'm sorry, Dad. I don't mean to be nosy or pushy. I'll shut up and back out. I can't help it; I'm just excited for you."

"That's okay." Seymour smiled at Chance. "It's all good."

Chance smiled back at him. "Good. I just don't want you feeling under any outside pressure. I know you'll be putting enough pressure on yourself."

Seymour shrugged and picked up the glass of bourbon he'd left on the bar when he'd gone over to see Chris. "I'm here to get away from the pressure for a while. Didn't you say that we could go and sit outside on the deck? I'd forgotten how beautiful this place is."

They made their way outside and took a seat. Seymour leaned back and took in the amazing view of the lake and mountains that surrounded it. He hadn't been back here since

Chance and Hope's wedding. It was a good place. He was hoping that it would do him and his life good to spend some time here.

Chapter Two

Chris finished folding the laundry and took it through to the bedroom. She set it down on the bed and frowned when she heard the doorbell. Who was that? She wasn't expecting anyone, and she'd been looking forward to having the morning to herself. This was the first day in a couple of weeks that she didn't have any appointments at the women's center, and she was glad of the break.

She forced a smile onto her face as she made her way to the front door and opened it. The smile became more genuine when she saw her daughter-in-law, Missy, standing there.

"Hey." Missy held up two ice cream cones and grinned. "I hope I'm not disturbing you, but I was walking back from town, and the ice cream truck was right there." She pointed at the street corner. "I had to get one, and I figured while I was this close, you might want one, too." She thrust one of the cones toward her.

Chris took it with a smile. "Thanks."

"And don't worry," said Missy, "I don't need to keep you if you're busy."

"No. I'm not busy. Come on in."

Missy followed her into the kitchen and pulled out one of the stools at the island. Once she was perched on it, she took a lick of her ice cream and wrinkled her nose. "So, what's going on with you?"

Chris gave her a shrewd look. "Why do I get the feeling that this visit is about more than ice cream?"

Missy tried to look innocent but failed miserably and laughed instead. "Because you know me too well, and you know how this town works. I told myself I could be subtle and not ask you anything, but you know me, I'm too good at being upfront. So, what's the deal? When are you going out with Seymour?"

Chris rolled her eyes. "I do know how this town works, but it still surprises me how fast gossip travels. And I have to tell you, I'm surprised at Chance; I didn't think he'd say anything."

Missy laughed. "He didn't. He wouldn't; ever. To say that we're brother and sister, we couldn't be more different. Chance didn't say a word, and neither did Hope. You've got Kenzie to thank for the whole world knowing that you and Seymour are about to be an item."

"I should have known. That little madam …"

"You know you love her, really. And it's not malicious. She was thrilled."

"Maybe so, but she still shouldn't be gossiping about people's private business."

Missy gave her a curious look. "You surprise me. I wouldn't have thought you'd mind people knowing."

Chris shrugged. Normally, she didn't mind people knowing her business. She wasn't a very private person, more of an open book.

Missy smiled. "So, why does it bother you? Is it because it's important to you?"

She shrugged again. "I don't really know why. I mean, to be fair, I've made no secret of the fact that I like him."

"Yeah, and it's been no secret when you've dated people before. But Seymour's different, right?"

Chris pursed her lips. "Not really. Maybe it's just because this has been such a long time in the making."

Missy looked like she wanted to say more, but instead, she took another lick of her ice cream. "So, when's the hot date?"

"I don't even know if there's going to be one yet. I don't know what Kenzie overheard; all I know is that we ran into each other at the Boathouse. He asked if I'd say yes if he asked me out to dinner. I told him I would, so he took my number and said he'd call me."

"And he hasn't called you yet?"

Chris laughed. "Don't look so disappointed, that was less than twenty-four hours ago."

"Oh, okay."

"But I hope he hurries up and calls soon. I feel like a schoolgirl waiting on her crush to call."

"Aww. I love that. And that's exactly what's happening, isn't it?"

Chris made a face. "I suppose. But my school days are a long way behind me, and I'd like to think that I had a bit more sense than that these days. Don't get me wrong. It'll be nice to go on a date, but it doesn't hold the same kind of importance as it did back then."

"It doesn't? Or you just think it shouldn't?"

Chris sighed. "It doesn't. Granted, I might want it to, but at my age, it's all so different. Back then, I was thinking about the rest of my life and finding the man to spend it with. Now I'm just thinking about one night in the next week and how much fun it might be to spend it with a man whose company I enjoy, instead of a game show host on the TV."

Missy narrowed her eyes. "Are you deliberately playing this down?"

"Maybe. I like the man. That's no secret, but come on, Missy, I'm a realist if nothing else. I know you girls are all so happy that you've found your happily ever afters that you'd like to set everyone around up with one of their own, but you're forgetting that I had mine—a long time ago. That's a young woman's dream. I'm more interested in making a new friend. Spending some time with a man whose company I enjoy," she waggled her eyebrows, "and maybe getting a little physical enjoyment out of the arrangement, too."

Missy pursed her lips.

"What?" Chris laughed. "Don't you dare look all disapproving at me like that. You might not like to think about it, but we oldies still have our desires, you know."

"Hey! I wasn't looking disapproving at that. Though I wouldn't want to be around if Jack heard you say it. I was pissed at you for thinking that's all you can have. You're saying there's no reason you shouldn't still be dating and having sex—I'm saying there's no reason you can't fall in love again and have a happily ever after—and one that's happy this time."

Chris shook her head. "It may be possible, but not for me."

"Why? Because you won't let it happen? That's the only reason I can see."

"No, because—" Chris was grateful when her phone rang and interrupted her. Missy might be right, but Chris didn't want to talk about it, because she didn't know what she thought about it. And anyway, it didn't matter because she had to answer her … Her heart started to race as she picked up her cell. It was a number she didn't recognize … was it him?

"Hello?"

"Hi Chris, this is Seymour."

She felt the heat in her cheeks as she looked at Missy. "Hi there."

"Hi. How are you?"

Missy raised her eyebrows and pointed at the phone. "Is it him?" she asked in a loud stage whisper.

Chris nodded. To her relief, Missy slid down from the stool and made her way to the door. She turned back when she reached it and held up her crossed fingers. Chris was relieved when she let herself out and closed the door behind her.

"Hello?"

Oops. She should have answered him, instead of making him wait till Missy had gone.

~ ~ ~

"Hi, sorry about that. Missy was just leaving when you called."

Seymour frowned to himself. She sounded flustered. "Is this a bad time? I can call back."

"No. Not at all. She's gone now. It's lovely to hear from you."

He relaxed a little. It'd been so long since he'd called a woman to ask her out that he'd been nervous about doing this. The sound of her voice reassured him. She was pleased he'd called, and so was he. "Okay. And Missy? She's Chance's sister, isn't she?"

"She is." He could hear that she was nervous, too, as she laughed. "I was thinking about that after I saw you yesterday. "Chance is your son-in-law; Missy is my daughter-in-law. Does that mean we're related somehow?"

He thought about it for a moment. "I don't think so. At least, not in any way that means we can't go out—if you still want to."

"I do. I'd like that. When were you thinking?"

"I'd like to say tonight, but we ran into Anne and Graham Hemming this morning, and they insisted on inviting me over to dinner. They're very old friends. Do you know them?"

"I do. Their son, Pete, is my Jack's best friend and business partner. They're lovely people. How do you know them?"

He held his breath for a moment, then had to clear his throat before he could answer. This was strange. This was why he didn't make the effort to get to know women or to date. It was why he hadn't made the effort to come and see Chris before now. "Kate" was the only word that came out when he finally made his voice work. He'd meant to say that they'd been his wife's friends.

"That's nice. I hope you have a good evening catching up with them."

"Thanks." He needed to pull himself together. "How about tomorrow? Are you free?"

"I am. Where would you like to go? We don't have much choice around here. There's the Boathouse or we could go over to the Lodge at Four Mile Creek or there's a little Italian place called Giuseppe's."

"Chance recommended Giuseppe's—if you like it there?"

"I do. The Lodge is all the way on the other side of the lake. The Boathouse is good, but …"

He chuckled. "I think I already figured out the problem with that place. If we go there, there'll be no hiding from prying eyes."

"That's right."

"Giuseppe's it is, then. What time is good for you?"

"Say seven? I'll meet you there?"

"I'll pick you up—if you like." He wasn't used to this. His mind was racing, considering all the angles. To his way of thinking, a guy was supposed to pick a girl up to take her out. But he hadn't done this in a long time. Maybe these days women preferred to make their own way? Maybe it was a safety consideration—so he didn't know where she lived. He smiled to himself while he waited for her answer. He needed to slow down.

"If it's not out of your way?"

"You'll have to tell me where you are first, but it's hardly going to be out of my way wherever it is. I'm staying at the resort."

"Okay." She gave him her address, and he wrote it down. "And don't worry if you want to have a glass of wine or two. We can always walk back. Giuseppe's isn't far."

He didn't like to tell her that it didn't matter if he had a drink; he wouldn't be the one driving. Ivan, his driver, was here with him. Now he stopped to think about it, it probably wasn't necessary, but it was just normal to him. Wherever he went, Ivan went, too. He hoped that wouldn't be an issue for her, but there was no need to bring it up now. "Okay."

He wanted to keep her on the phone, wanted to talk to her, maybe even suggest that they shouldn't wait till tomorrow night—that they should go out and get some lunch right now.

He looked out the window at the lake. But no. "Well, I'll see you tomorrow at seven then."

"I'll look forward to it."

He hung up and sighed. He should have asked. But it was too late now. He'd just have to wait. He looked around the cabin. It was nice enough, not his usual kind of place, but Hope and Chance stayed here whenever they came to the lake, and this time, they'd booked another cabin for him. He should just relax and enjoy himself, maybe sit out on the porch and take in the view. He didn't feel like sitting around and relaxing, though. It wasn't his way. He looked over at his computer, which was sitting on the dining table. He could get a few hours work in while Hope and Chance were visiting their friends. But no. He knew part of Hope's motivation for bringing him with them was to make him take a break from work. He'd promised her that he wouldn't spend the whole time with his nose in his laptop, and he was a man of his word.

He went into the kitchen and looked around, opening and closing cupboards as he went. Then he smiled. Hope wanted him to relax and do something that wasn't work, and now he knew what he could do. He could bake! He could go up to the grocery store that he'd seen in town and get what he needed and have cookies ready by the time she and Chance came back. He picked up his phone to call Ivan, then set it down again. He could at least walk over to Ivan's cabin.

~ ~ ~

Chris picked up a basket and wandered over to the produce section. She deliberately hadn't gotten anything in for dinner— in case Seymour called and asked her out. Now at least she knew that their date was happening, but she still had to find something for tonight.

She felt like a salad. After that ice cream Missy had brought her this afternoon, she didn't need anything too heavy. She picked up a tomato to feel how ripe it was and almost squashed it when she saw Seymour walking toward her. He hadn't noticed her. He was too busy studying the list in his hand. She wondered if she should just let him go by. No! Why would she? She could be called many things, but a shrinking violet wasn't one of them.

"What are you doing here?" she called.

He looked up from his list and looked around, obviously unsure if someone was addressing him or someone else.

"Seymour," she waved her tomato at him.

That caught his eye, and he smiled and came to her. "Hello! This is a nice surprise. I didn't think I'd see you until tomorrow."

"Neither, did I, but a girl has to eat tonight, too."

He looked at the tomato she was still clutching.

She felt foolish. "I wouldn't have expected to see you here, though."

"Oh." He held up his list, looking a little sheepish. "Yes. I don't need to make dinner, but I wanted to make ..." He looked embarrassed, and she felt bad for putting him on the spot.

He let out a small laugh. "Don't look like that. It's nothing too shameful, though I'm probably making it sound that way." He showed her his list. "I'm making cookies." He shrugged. "I'm not the most domesticated person on earth, but these last couple of years I've been trying my hand at all kinds of things. I'm pretty good at cookies."

"Good for you!" Chris didn't know what else to say. She wanted to hug him. He'd gone from looking embarrassed to looking proud of himself. It was such an unexpected confession; it made her heart melt a little bit.

"I'll bring you some tomorrow if you like."

"Thank you. I'll look forward to sampling your talents."

His chin jerked up, and he met her gaze for a moment before looking away.

Oh, no! He didn't think she'd meant something else by that, did he? From the look on his face, she'd guess that he thought she meant a very different kind of talent. If the truth were told, she wouldn't mind—but she'd hardly suggest it out of the blue in the produce aisle of the grocery store!

She looked at her watch as if she were in some kind of hurry. "And on that note. I'd better get going. I'll see you tomorrow."

She hurried away from him, still clutching her tomato and headed for the laundry aisle, where she was fairly certain he wouldn't come looking for chocolate chips.

Seymour smiled to himself as he watched her walk away. He had a feeling she knew full well how that had sounded. His smile faded. He hadn't tested his talents in that department in a long while. Still, he was confident he wouldn't be too rusty. The way her backside swayed from side to side as she hurried to the end of the aisle made him want to find out. He looked down at his list. Back to the business at hand. For now, he needed to buy the ingredients and get back to making his cookies. He'd save some for her. And he already knew that they were the only kind of dessert he'd be indulging in with her tomorrow night, but maybe ... He drew in a deep breath and slowly let it out. Maybe one day they'd get to that stage.

For now, he didn't need to get ahead of himself. This would be his first date in a couple of years. That was enough to navigate without thinking about where it might go in the future—or even if it might go anywhere.

Chris was fun. She was a breath of fresh air. He wanted to get to know her better. But that didn't mean anything. She might find him too stuffy, too driven, too work-focused. He'd been working on the stuffy thing. He didn't know how not to be driven, and the work focus? That was the only focus he'd had or wanted in his life after Kate died. It was only in the last couple of years that he'd managed to open up to his own daughter. How was he supposed to focus on a new woman in his life?

He reached the baking aisle and stopped. He was getting way too far ahead of himself. One step at a time. The first step would be tomorrow night. They'd have dinner, maybe they'd find the attraction wore off over the course of the evening. If not, they could take another step. Right now, the only step that needed his focus was to find the chocolate chips.

Chapter Three

Chris looked herself over in the mirror in the hallway. "Not bad," she said with a smile. "Not bad at all." She'd never understood women who struggled with their own image. As far as Chris was concerned, everyone was beautiful in their own way. You just had to figure out what your way was and make the most of it.

She considered herself fortunate that she'd inherited her mom's dark hair and complexion and hour-glass figure. Her sister, Marianne, was slimmer; she always had been. When they were growing up, Chris had envied her that, but as she'd matured, she'd learned to be grateful for her own curves.

She looked at the clock in the living room. It was only six-forty, but she was all ready to go. If Seymour hadn't said he'd pick her up, she'd be leaving now—and that would still put her at the restaurant ten minutes early. It was just her way. She picked up her purse and looked inside. She had everything she might need—except, oops, that wasn't like her. When she'd been gathering her things earlier, she'd slipped her wallet inside—and it was the wrong one. She hurried upstairs and fetched the matching wallet from the shelf in her closet. She had a collection. Most of her wallets matched her purses; she liked to buy sets. Some weren't exactly matched, but she still knew which went with which. Her sister teased her about that little detail sometimes—and about many others. But to Chris, it was important. She wasn't sloppy; she wasn't careless.

She sat down at the kitchen table and transferred the contents of her wallet into the new one, then slipped it into her purse. And now it was six-forty-five. She smiled. She liked this time; she saw it as time that she'd earned. It was her little bubble, the ten or fifteen minutes she bought herself by being ready in advance. It meant she got to arrive places early and observe the people around her, or times like tonight, it meant she got to sit with her thoughts for a little while and check in with herself.

She pushed her hair back from her face. How was she tonight? She smiled. She was good. She was excited, thrilled to finally be going on this date that she and Seymour had talked about back in LA. She was a little nervous—she liked Seymour. She hoped he liked her, too. She was hoping that this might be their first date. But if it turned out to be their only date, she'd live. It'd be another experience that she'd collected along this journey that was life. It was like she'd told Missy yesterday; she wasn't looking for someone to share life with, just someone to share some time with.

Some laughs, hopefully. Some stories. She already knew from that first night they met that they shared some life experience. They'd each raised their children alone after their spouse died. She sighed. Seymour had loved his wife very much. They'd led a happy life together from what he'd told her. She, on the other hand ... well, her marriage hadn't been such a happy one. She'd loved him. She'd been devasted when he drank himself into an early grave, but she still carried the guilt—the guilt that came with relief. Even now, all these years later, it was hard to admit that she'd been relieved when he died. Still. She sat up a little bit straighter. She liked to believe that he'd been a good a man. A good man who'd been eaten alive by his demons and his addiction.

She got up from the table. She didn't like to dwell. She'd managed to turn it all around in her mind. She liked to believe that now he was free of his demons and that he'd be happy for her and the boys if he were looking down on them. She hoped he'd found the peace in death that had eluded him in life.

"Okay," she said out loud. "That was yesterday. This is today." She went to close the living room curtains. It was too early, yet, but she didn't like to leave them open when she was out in the evening.

She stopped with her hand raised when she saw an SUV pull up outside. It wasn't one of the neighbors; she knew all their cars. It looked like there were two men inside. She frowned. Summer Lake was a quiet little place; nothing bad ever happened here, but she felt uneasy. She moved back from the window, wondering if she should call Colt. He was one of Jack and Dan's friends—and the deputy sheriff. It might not be a bad idea to let him know there was a strange vehicle. "Oh!" She suddenly felt foolish as she saw Seymour get out of the passenger side. He leaned back in and spoke to the driver before closing the door.

She went into the hallway and waited for the bell to ring before she opened the door with a smile. She'd had a quip ready to tell him how she'd been about to call the police on the strange man outside, but it died in her throat at the sight of him. He took her breath away. His eyes were mesmerizing. She'd thought they were hazel, but as he stood there on the doorstep smiling at her, she could see they were a deep green. Her heart raced as she returned the smile.

"Sorry, I know I'm a little early. It's a habit I can't seem to break. I was going to sit outside and wait for a few minutes, but I thought that might look as though we were prowlers casing the neighborhood."

She laughed. "I'm glad you changed your mind. I'm ready—I'm always early, too. And I was just debating whether I should call in the suspicious vehicle outside my house. Do you want to come in for a minute?"

"Sure." He looked back at the SUV before following her inside.

"I'll just get my purse—unless you'd like a drink? Who's that in the car? He can join us if you like?"

Seymour shook his head. "That's okay. That's Ivan. He's my driver."

Chris raised an eyebrow at him. "Your driver? You don't drive?"

She couldn't figure out the look on his face. "I can drive, but I don't. I ..." He pursed his lips and looked away. "I have a driver. I have a pilot, too." He looked back at her with a smile. "You know what I do for a living."

She nodded. She couldn't claim to understand what he did, but she knew he was involved in the investment world. He ran a hedge fund and did some other stuff. She'd seen him on the news being interviewed when there was big news about the markets.

"I work a lot. I work most of the time. Every hour that I put into my work produces a lot of money. So, I dedicate my time to doing what I do best, and I hire people to do the things that don't require my attention."

She cocked her head to one side and held his gaze for a moment.

"You disapprove?" he asked eventually.

"No. Oh, my goodness no. I'm not judging. It's not my place to judge. I'm just trying to figure you out. I can't imagine what it's like. I can't imagine letting someone else drive me around.

But then I don't have anything more important—or more profitable—to do with my time. It's just a logical arrangement to you, isn't it?"

He nodded. "When you run the numbers, you can see that it makes sense. If I can make one thousand dollars in an hour either on the phone or on my laptop while sitting in the back of the car in traffic, and I can pay Ivan one hundred dollars to drive while I do it. I'd be crazy not to. It'd be like paying nine hundred dollars an hour to drive myself."

Chris had to laugh at that. It made sense, but she would never have thought of it that way. "If the rate's one hundred an hour, you can leave him at home next time you come up here, and I'll drive."

He looked uncomfortable. "I was only illustrating—"

She reached out and touched his arm. "And I'm only joking with you. I don't even know if you'll be coming here again—and if you do, I'll happily drive you around for free."

He smiled. "Sorry. I guess I'm a little on edge. When you said we could walk home later if I wanted to have a drink, I wondered if I should tell you about Ivan then. I didn't know if it'd seem strange to you. If you'd mind. Do you mind?"

"Of course not. And it's not so strange. Did you know that my sister, Marianne, is engaged to Clay McAdam?"

He smiled. "I knew Clay got engaged, but I had no idea that it was to your sister."

"Yeah. I'm so glad they found each other. They make each other happy. Anyway, my point was that Clay has a couple of guys, Adam and Davin, who drive him around—they're like bodyguards, too. His security team. I get along well with them." She stopped and frowned at him. "Is Ivan just your driver, or is he security, too?"

"Both. Not that I need security for any particular reason, but you never know."

She looked at him for a long moment. She'd been about to ask him why he might need security, but she got lost in his eyes. Now they were a light brown, flecked with green. They might just be the most beautiful eyes she'd ever seen.

His lips quirked up into a smile as if he knew the effect he was having on her. "Anything else you want to know?"

"Only if you want to have a drink here or if you'd like to go?" She could hardly ask him any of the questions that were racing through her mind, none of them were appropriate for a first date.

"Maybe we should go."

The way he said it made her wonder if he was having the same kind of thoughts she was. She picked up her purse and led him to the front door. Maybe she was just getting a bit carried away.

~ ~ ~

Seymour looked around as they followed the server to their table. Giuseppe's wasn't the kind of place he'd normally frequent, but he liked it. It felt warm and welcoming.

When they reached the table, the server set two menus down on the table. "I'll be back to take your drink orders in a few," he said with a smile.

Seymour pursed his lips and pulled out a chair for Chris.

She sat down and smiled at him as he joined her. "Thank you, but don't be mad at the kid for not doing it. It's just how things work these days."

He blew out a sigh. "Was it that obvious that I wasn't impressed?"

"I don't think he noticed, but then he wouldn't have a clue what you were pissed about. It wouldn't have occurred to him that he should do it."

"You're right. I'm sorry, I guess I'm old school in that respect. But I shouldn't get annoyed at people for not living up to expectations they don't even know I have."

Chris laughed. "I think we're all guilty of that in one way or another."

He smiled. "You're probably right about that. I hope you'll let me know what your expectations are."

"I've learned not to have many. It makes life easier. I prefer to take things as they come."

He held her gaze for a moment. He wanted to tell her that it was better to have some expectations and hold people accountable to them, but she'd already proved her point with the server.

She gave him a playful smile. "Do you have certain expectations of me? I wouldn't want to piss you off."

He laughed. "No, I don't. At least, nothing that I'm aware of."

"Good, then, although I'd guess that it doesn't come naturally to you, I'd like to suggest that that you take things as they come this evening."

"Just for this evening?" Had she already decided that that was as long as she could put up with him?

She laughed. "If we're playing this by ear, then we won't know if what I think will matter to you after this evening, will we?"

He nodded. "You're right. We won't. But I've built my life and made people's fortunes on my ability to make predictions. And I'd predict that what you think will still matter to me tomorrow."

She held his gaze for a moment, then smiled at the server who'd returned to see what they wanted to drink.

"So, why now?" asked Chris after he'd gone.

Seymour raised an eyebrow. He thought he knew what she meant, but he wanted to buy himself a few moments to consider his answer.

"I just wondered why you finally decided to come up to the lake." She smiled. "Why we're sitting here right now. You don't have to answer if you don't want to, or if you don't know."

He smiled. "It'd be easier to mumble something about the time seeming right, but you deserve the truth."

It was Chris's turn to raise an eyebrow. "That sounds ominous. Are you sure I want to know?"

He laughed. "I think you do. You see, after that night we met in LA." He stopped and pondered the wisdom of being as honest as he was about to be. He realized that it wasn't his wisdom, but his courage that was in question. That made it easier to go on. "I wanted to call you the next day. I wanted to come up here and see you, to continue laying the foundation I thought we'd started to build." He shrugged. "But I managed to talk myself out of it."

"Why?"

"Because I've gotten too good at hiding. Hiding from life, hiding from reality. Hiding from happiness."

She cocked her head to one side. It was adorable the way she did that.

"You want to know why I'd hide from happiness?"

She gave a little chuckle. "No, that's not what puzzles me. I get that part. I guess I'm more surprised that you thought your happiness might be at stake if you got in touch with me."

"We both knew there was a possibility of something very real between us." His heart was hammering in his chest. He hadn't intended to be this open, but he couldn't help it, something about her demanded absolute honesty.

"I thought there was, but I wasn't sure you even wanted to consider it."

"I did, and that scared me. I thought my way through all the logical routes that this could go. I reached the conclusion that we could likely find happiness together. I wasn't sure I could handle that."

She smiled. "Which brings me back to my original question—what makes you want to find out now?"

He blew out a sigh and reached across the table to take hold of her hand. Her eyes widened, but she didn't pull away. "Because I've finally run out of excuses not to. I've managed to escape almost everything I didn't want to deal with in life by hiding in my work. But you …" He squeezed her hand and smiled. "I can't hide from you. You somehow took up residence in my head. You make me want to know what it'd be like to allow myself to be happy."

She held his gaze for a long moment. She looked serious, doubtful, maybe, but eventually, she smiled. "I think you deserve to be happy. I think it'd do you good to relax and have some fun—maybe not work so much. I think I can help you with that."

He waited, it sounded like there was a but coming.

"If you're going to stay here until next weekend, then maybe I can be the catalyst you need."

He frowned. That wasn't what he meant. He wasn't looking for some vacation fling. "I'm not here to—"

She held up her hand to stop him. "I think I know what you mean. But if we're playing this by ear, then even next weekend is a long way away. Don't you think?"

He wasn't used to playing things by ear. He didn't work that way. Yes, he adjusted on the fly to changing circumstances, but he always knew where he was headed, what his end goal was in any endeavor.

Chris squeezed his hand. "I can see cogs whirring behind those pretty eyes of yours. Slow down, would you? Let's have dinner, have fun, get to know each other, and that's all tonight needs to be. If we have fun, we have another ten days or so to play with before you leave."

He nodded slowly. "Is that all you want? Some fun?"

Her smile faded. "Honestly?"

"I should warn you; honesty is one of my expectations."

"Okay, then to be as blunt as I can. It's all about fun. My life is good. I have my kids, my grandkids, the causes I support. I'm okay. If I can layer a little fun over the top of that, then that will be wonderful. I'm not greedy. I'm not asking for more than that."

He wondered if she was trying to reassure him that she wasn't going to ask too much of him, or if she was trying to warn him that he shouldn't ask too much of her. "And if I were to ask for more than that?"

"You won't—"

He started to interrupt, but she held up her hand again with a smile. "You won't even know if you want to ask for more for a while yet." She chuckled. "For all you know you might be calling that pilot of yours to get you out of here and away from that annoying Chris woman long before next weekend rolls around. That's why I'm saying play it by ear."

He had to smile. "I'm sorry. I know you're right. I'll try to back off."

"I'm not asking you to back off. All I'm saying is that we can have fun with this—and we don't need to try to make it into anything more than that."

"What if it turns into more than that all by itself?"

She laughed. "Then we'll be onto something, won't we? But if we try to plan it and manage it from the beginning it won't do anything all by itself, will it?"

"Are you ready to order?"

They both looked up at the server who was staring pointedly at the menus which still lay on the table where he'd left them.

"I'll call you over when we are." Seymour tried not to scowl at him, but it was hard.

When he'd gone, Chris laughed and handed Seymour a menu. "Here, I recommend the pizza, it's wonderful."

He made himself relax and smile back at her. "Okay. Pizza it is."

Chapter Four

Chris couldn't believe it when she set her glass down and looked at her watch. It was just after eleven! They'd been sitting here for four hours. No wonder the poor server had been giving them the evil eye for a while now. She looked around. The restaurant was almost empty. She hadn't noticed.

Seymour smiled at her. "You're right. We should go."

"I don't want to." She laughed. "I wasn't giving you a hint that it's time to get out of here. I was just shocked. Where did the time go?"

"I have no idea. But I enjoyed it."

"I did, too." She reached across the table and took hold of his hand. He'd taken hold of hers a few times throughout the evening. It felt natural. "I had a really good time. Thank you."

"I'd thought we could go for a walk down by the lake afterward, but it's a bit late now."

"I'm allowed to stay out as late as I want. We can still do that—unless you're tired?"

"No. I'd love to. Do you want Ivan to drive us back over to the resort?"

She waved a hand at him. "No. Let him go home. I'd planned to say that earlier, you should let him know he can have the rest of the night off."

"Don't worry. I didn't make him sit outside all this time. He's back at his cabin. I said I'd call when I needed him."

"Why don't you call him now and tell him that you don't need him?"

"Okay."

She watched as he fished his phone out of his pocket. "Ivan … No. Thanks. We're going to walk back … Okay."

Chris waved her hand in front of Seymour's face. He gave her a puzzled look, and it occurred to her that he wasn't used to people doing anything like that to him. She smiled and held her hand out for the phone. "Can I have a word with him?"

Two vertical lines appeared between his brows, but he nodded. "Hold on, Ivan. Chris would like to speak to you."

"Hey, Ivan. I'm sorry we didn't call you earlier. You could have had the night off."

"That's okay."

"I just wanted to let you know that if you walk up to the restaurant at the resort—the Boathouse, have you seen it?"

"I have."

"Well, if you take a walk up there, I'm sure it'll still be busy. You should enjoy yourself. Go see the bartender—the blonde girl, her name is Kenzie. Tell her I sent you and that your drinks are on me."

"No. You don't need to do that. Though I appreciate the offer."

"Please do. I hate to think of you sitting home twiddling your thumbs all night. You should go out and have some fun."

She could hear the smile in his voice when he spoke again. "It's kind of you to think of me. I might take a walk up there, but I can get my own tab."

"At least let Kenzie know who you are? She'll introduce you to the locals—you may as well make some friends while you're here."

"Thanks."

Chris looked at Seymour. His lips were quirking up in that odd little smile. "Anyway," she said to Ivan. "I'll let you go. I'll give you back to Seymour now." She handed the phone back to him.

He brought it up to his ear with the same smile. "You should go … I won't call you before noon tomorrow. Yes. Goodnight, Ivan." He ended the call and looked at Chris. "Thank you."

"What for?"

"For thinking of him like that. For telling him to go out and have some fun."

She narrowed her eyes. "I hope you're not mean to him?"

He laughed. "Of course not. At least, not intentionally so, but you just made me realize that maybe I expect too much of him. I forget that not everyone sees their work the same way I do. I should cut him some slack in the future."

"How do you see your work?"

He shrugged. "I tend to wear blinders. It's not so much how I see my work, as that I only see my work, everything else is secondary—to be fit in around the edges."

"I see."

His smile faded. "I've been working on changing that, though," he added hurriedly.

Chris had to laugh. "Don't worry. I'm not judging."

"I didn't think you were. I was trying to let you know that I'd like to make more room in my life for things other than work. For …"

She wondered what he was about to say, but he seemed to change his mind. He smiled. "I have been doing better lately. In fact, why don't we get out of here?"

She watched as he called the server to bring the check.

After he'd paid, they made their way outside, and Chris set off back toward town. They walked in silence for a few minutes before she felt him slip his fingers around hers.

She looked up at him and smiled.

"Is this okay?" He brought their joined hands up in front of them, making her laugh.

"It's very okay. I like it."

"Good." He let their hands drop down between their sides again as they carried on walking. "I like it, too. I had a good time tonight, Chris."

"I did too. I can't believe that we sat there for four hours!"

"I know. I thought I had it all figured out earlier. I thought we'd spend two to two and a half hours over dinner, then we'd walk on the beach, and then perhaps a nightcap at the Boathouse before I saw you home."

She laughed. "It sounds like we had a similar plan. I'm happy that we surprised ourselves, though."

"Yes, this is so much better. We weren't working to a schedule; we were just enjoying ourselves. I'd almost forgotten how to do that."

She laughed. "You stick with me, then. I'll remind you how to have fun."

~ ~ ~

Her eyes shone as she smiled up at him. She was beautiful. His heart beat a little faster at her words. Stick with her? The way he felt right now, he'd love to. But he could only stick with what she'd said earlier about playing this by ear.

"I'd love to take you up on that offer. Fun hasn't been high on my priority list."

She pursed her lips. "I already figured that out. You know what they say about all work and no play, don't you?"

He held her gaze for a moment. He didn't mind admitting that he'd been too intensely focused on his work, but he didn't want her to go getting the idea that he was dull. He dropped his gaze to her lips for a moment and then looked back up into her eyes. "Just because it hasn't been on my priority list, doesn't mean I've forgotten how."

Her eyes widened a little, but there was a definite sparkle to them when she spoke again. "Good to know. And before we left the restaurant, you said that you'd been getting better at doing things that aren't work. What have you getting up to?"

He wasn't sure if she was changing the subject away from the kind of fun they might have—or if she wanted to know how much of that fun he'd been getting. He smiled. "I shared one of my dirty little secrets with you yesterday."

She raised an eyebrow.

"I don't suppose many people would think of baking cookies as a dirty little secret, but it's so far out of my lane, that it kind of feels that way."

"Aww." She squeezed his hand, which he'd forgotten she was holding as they walked; it felt so natural. "Aren't you sweet? The big busy businessman allowing himself to be so vulnerable as to bake cookies."

He gave her a puzzled look. "Vulnerable?"

"Hell, yes! Stepping outside your comfort zone? Trying something you don't expect to be good at? Being prepared to fail at something you know other people can do with ease? Yeah. I'd say that's allowing yourself to be vulnerable." She winked at him. "And I'd also say that—for some strange reason—it's kind of hot."

He laughed. "Baking cookies is hot? Do you have some kind of kitchen fetish?"

She laughed with him. "No. I really don't. Kitchens don't do much for me. But trust me. There's something about it that … I don't know."

"Are you sure you're not just teasing me? Do you think it's sad and you're not telling me?"

She laughed again. "No! I do not. I'm serious. There's something sexy about the thought of you in the kitchen—"

He raised an eyebrow. "Is it the rolling pin?"

"Oh, my God! No!" She couldn't stop laughing now. When she finally managed to, she waggled her eyebrows at him. "Though now you mention it, what do you get up to with the rolling pin?"

He held his hands up. "I have no idea! I thought you knew something I didn't."

"No. Although, I can tell you that my imagination will be running wild with that one."

Seymour watched her as they walked on. She was quite something. He loved that she was so open and honest with him, and so prepared to laugh with him—and at him.

"You've got me wondering what you'll think about my other attempts at having fun now."

"Try me. The baking thing definitely earns you some brownie points—if you'll forgive the pun."

He groaned. "I will, but only this once."

She shrugged. "Sometimes they fall flat. Go on, what else do you do in your attempts to have fun and not work yourself to death?"

He smiled. "I don't think you'll find anything sexy about this one, but it's much more important to me than baking cookies."

"What is it?"

"Playing with my grandson."

The way she smiled, he knew she understood the joy that brought him.

"Aww! He's a little angel, isn't he?"

Seymour nodded. "He is. He makes me see life through new eyes."

"They'll do that to you."

"You have a granddaughter, don't you? And earlier you said your grandkids—plural?"

"Yes. Isabel is my eldest son, Jack's. He and his wife Emma are trying for another one. And then there's Scott. My younger boy, Dan, he's married to Missy. Well, Missy had Scott when she was just a teenager. Scott never knew his father, but since Dan came into their lives, he's become Scott's dad—and I've become his grandma. He's a good boy."

"He's the computer kid, isn't he? Chance has talked about him."

"That's right. Scotty loves his Uncle Chance. They're an unlikely pair—the cowboy and the geek is how Scott says it, but they're close."

Seymour smiled. "That's good."

"It is, Chance is a good guy. He might have his rough edges, but he has a heart of gold."

"I know it. When I first heard that my daughter was running with some no-good ranch hand, I was ready to run him off—buy him off—whatever it took to get him out of her life."

"I'm glad you took the time to get to know him before you did that."

"So am I. I don't mind admitting when I'm wrong. And I couldn't have been more wrong about Chance. I'm proud to call him my son-in-law, and I can rest easy knowing that my daughter found herself a good man."

"Here we are."

Seymour had been so involved in their conversation that he
hadn't noticed how far they'd walked. They'd just turned a
corner and were in the square in the center of the resort, just
outside the Boathouse. He was sad their walking and talking
would come to an end now.

"Do you want to get a drink?"

"I thought you promised me a walk on the beach?"

He smiled. "So I did. How do we get there?"

She pointed across the square. There are steps over there.
It's just the small, town beach, but it's probably too late to
head to the main beach."

"Maybe we can walk there another day?" He already knew he
wanted to see her again.

She smiled. "Any day you like."

"How about tomorrow?"

She nodded. "We can if you're that keen. I'm at the center in
the morning, but I'm free in the afternoon."

"I am that keen. I don't see any point in hiding it. I thought
if anyone was supposed to play hard to get, it was the woman."

She laughed. "I guess it is, but you won't get any of that
from me. I was never into games, and I'm too old to start
playing them now."

"Good."

They reached the steps and made their way down them.
Seymour was surprised to find his feet sinking into the sand.

"Are you okay?"

"Yes. I don't know why but I thought it'd be a pebble
beach."

"It should be, but Ben—the guy who owns the resort—
brought in some sand a couple of summers ago and it was a
big hit with the visitors."

"That makes sense."

"But you don't like it? You don't want to get sand in your shoes?"

He made a face at her. "Are you trying to make out I don't know how to have fun?"

She laughed. "No, just that you might want to loosen up a little."

"You might be right." He thought about it, but only for a moment before he slid his arms around her waist and lifted her off her feet, running the short distance to the water's edge with her. He swung her out over the water, and she clung to him.

"You wouldn't dare!" she gasped through her laughter.

"Wouldn't I?" he asked with a laugh. "Don't you think it'd be fun?"

She laughed and wrapped her arms tighter around his neck. "Don't do it!"

He swung her feet back down onto the sand and smiled down at her. "Don't worry. I wouldn't."

Her arms were still around his neck, and he tightened his around her waist, drawing her closer until they were touching from knees to chests. Her eyes shone as she looked up into his. As he lowered his head, he wasn't sure if it was his heart he could feel hammering against his chest or hers. He stopped when his lips were an inch from hers. He wanted so badly to kiss her, but he needed to know that it was what she wanted, too.

She gave him the answer as her fingers slid up into his hair, pulling him down to close the gap between them. He'd only intended a brief kiss, a declaration of interest, but the moment his lips came down on hers a shot of adrenaline coursed through him. It swept through her, too. There was no tentative beginning, there was only a shared hunger that they each tried to sate—lips crushing against each other, tongues exploring, hands roving. He'd thought this first kiss would be tentative, unhurried; instead, it was demanding. He slid his hands into her hair, tilting her head back to give him better access as he kissed her deeply. Her hands came down, from his shoulders, sliding around his waist, closing around his ass and pulling him against her in a move that only ignited him further.

When he finally lifted his head, he looked down into her eyes and let out a low whistle. "Wow! I wasn't expecting that."

She shook her head. "I sure as hell wasn't. And I thought you were such a gentleman."

He froze. Had his attraction to her made him go too far too fast. "I can be."

She chuckled. "Please don't."

That made him laugh. "You're definitely going to keep me on my toes, Chris."

She nodded. "I'll do my best. I'll play with you. Remind you how to have some fun."

Seymour was glad of the dark to cover his frown. To his mind, that kiss proved there was a whole lot more than fun at stake here.

She rubbed her hand up and down his arm. "I can hear those cogs whirring again, Seymour. I felt that just as much as you did, but I don't think we need to deviate from the plan. We have some fun—whatever else happens, or doesn't happen, we'll just have to wait and see.

Chapter Five

Chris watched Abbie walk out of the women's center and shook her head sadly.

"What's wrong?" asked Renée.

"It just makes me sad. Abbie could do so much with her life, but she refuses to leave this place."

"Her family's been through a lot. She doesn't want to leave her mom. I admire her for that."

Chris made a face. "You might see it differently when you have kids of your own. Yes, Abbie's a kind, caring person and it's admirable that she wants to be here for her mom. But that isn't a child's purpose in life. They're supposed to go out and spread their wings and live their own life. Her mom's not helpless or hopeless. And if Abbie wasn't here for her to lean on, she'd have to figure it out for herself and stand on her own two feet."

"Want to tell me what's really bothering you?" asked Renée.

Chris laughed. "It irks me that her mother will allow her to stay. My boys wanted to stay close by me. Did I want them to? Of course, I did. Was I scared what I'd do after they left? Damned straight I was. But their happiness, their futures, were more important to me. No way was I going to let them give up their dreams to take care of me. I just don't understand how Abbie's mom can do that to her."

"Have you ever thought that maybe she's not as strong or as brave as you?"

"Pft! That's my point. I'm not that brave or that strong, not really. The strength I had was the love of my kids." She shrugged. "I'm sorry. It's not my place to judge. It's only my place to support Abbie in whatever she chooses to do."

"And what's she choosing?"

"To stay here. To keep living with her mom and paying the bills."

"And how can we support her with that?"

"I sent her to see Megan. I heard Michael's looking to hire a new receptionist. Abbie would be perfect. She's good with people."

Renée smiled. "That sounds like it could work out well."

"Yeah. Not as well as her getting her butt out of this town and starting over somewhere, maybe going to school and ..." Chris stopped and lowered her hand, which she realized she'd been waving around as she spoke. She tended to do that when she got agitated. She gave Renée a rueful smile. "What do I know?"

"You know plenty. But none of us can know what's best for someone else. All we can do is support them to make their own decisions. Even when we don't agree with them. Do you want a coffee?"

Chris checked her watch. She had plenty of time before Seymour was due to come over. "I'd love one."

They walked through the doors that separated the women's center from the bakery. Renée owned and ran them both. Chris had a feeling that busy as the bakery was, most of its proceeds went to funding the women's center.

"Do you want to take a seat and I'll bring the coffees?"

"As long as you let me get you a pastry of some kind to go with it," said Chris. "And please don't turn me down, because I really want a brownie, but I won't eat one alone."

Renée laughed. "You've got yourself a deal. I'd never turn down a brownie. I'll bring them out."

She went behind the counter to pour the coffees, and Chris took a seat at a table by the window. She liked to watch the world go by. Main Street was always busy around lunchtime, and she liked to see who was out and about. She frowned when she saw a very familiar figure striding down the sidewalk toward the bakery. She made a face when he stopped at the bakery door and came in.

"Hey, Jack," Renée called from behind the counter. "What can I get you?"

Chris had a feeling he wasn't here to buy pastries.

Her suspicions were confirmed when he turned and scanned the tables and chairs. There were only a few people here. His glance skimmed over them until he spotted her. She smiled and waved at him. He nodded but didn't smile back.

"That's okay, thanks, Renée. I need a quick word with Mom."

He came over and bent down to kiss her cheek. "Mom."

"Jack." She tried to hide her smile but couldn't manage it. He was a good boy. She was so proud of him and all he'd achieved. It made her heart happy that her son was a respected member of the community; a leader if you like, and people looked up to him. But he was still her little boy. She knew why he wanted to talk to her, and she wasn't going to take any of his nonsense.

He tried to frown at her, but there was no hiding the smile in his big brown eyes. "How are you?"

"I'm fine, thank you. And how are you?" She tried not to laugh.

He narrowed his eyes at her. "You're not going to make this easy for me, are you?"

"Make what easy?" She tried her best to look innocent but knew that she wasn't pulling it off.

Jack blew out a sigh. "Want to tell me what's going on with you and Seymour Davenport?"

"Not particularly, no."

She smiled at Renée, who came and set down two cups of coffee for them. "I won't be long," she told her.

"You take your time," said Renée. "I'm here all day."

"I don't have all day," said Jack when she'd gone.

Chris laughed. "So, get back to work then, or wherever it is you need to go. I'm not keeping you here."

"Mom!"

"Yes, dear?"

Jack had to laugh. "I know it's none of my business. But I care, okay? I worry about you. Surely you can understand that? I just want to know that you're okay. You know what this town's like. There are rumors flying around about you and Seymour."

"So?"

Jack scowled. "So. What's going on?"

She liked to tease him. He was overly protective of her. She loved that he cared so much and that he looked out for her, but she wasn't going to let him overstep the mark. "Not that it's any of your business, but I had dinner with him last night. You shouldn't be surprised. You've known ever since LA that I liked him and that if he ever came up here, we'd go out."

"I know. And I'm not trying to be an asshole. I'm really not."

She chuckled. "It just comes naturally when you think about your mom having a life of her own?"

"That's not fair. I want you to have a life of your own. I just want it to be a happy one. And I want to know that if a guy is going to be part of it that he's a good guy."

"Well, I can assure you that Seymour is a very good guy. I think you'll like him. And if you don't want to take my word for it, ask Chance. The two of them have grown very close."

Jack sighed. "I already have asked Chance—and everyone else who knows him even a little bit. He had dinner with Pete's parents the other night."

"And have you heard anything that makes you wary of him?" Chris already knew the answer to that.

"No. By all accounts, he's a great guy."

"Well, then. What are you so worried about?"

"You!"

She laughed. "You're a very smart, very logical man, Jack. Except when it comes to me. I love that you want to protect me. But don't you think you're being just a teeny bit ridiculous?"

He scowled at her for a long moment, but she just smiled back at him. Eventually, his scowl faded, and they both ended up laughing. "I don't think I'm being a teeny bit ridiculous. I know I'm being full-on ridiculous. But I can't help it, Mom. When I think about someone hurting you, I lose it. I forget that I'm supposed to be smart and logical and I go all caveman."

"I know, sweetheart. And I love that you care about me. But it makes me sad, too."

"I'm sorry. I'd never want to—"

She held up her hand to stop him. "I don't mean that you make me sad by being so overprotective. I'm sad because I know what made you that way."

She could see the telltale pulse in his jaw. "I know we don't talk about it, but maybe one day we should?"

"No. There's no need."

"Okay. If you don't want to, we won't. But I do need to say that I'm sorry. I'm sorry your childhood wasn't what it could have been."

He held her gaze for a long moment. "It wasn't your fault. You did everything you could to make it better for us."

"True. But I couldn't do enough. You grew up too fast and tried to put yourself in charge of taking care of Dan and me. You should never have had to do that. I didn't want that for you."

He blew out a sigh. "It's okay, Mom. I wouldn't change … that's not true. I'd change a lot of it if I could. But I can't. So, instead, I choose to take what I can from it all. I wouldn't be who I am today if he hadn't been who he was."

Chris nodded sadly. "That's true. I just wish I could have protected you more."

Jack smiled. "And yet you're still complaining about me trying to protect you now?"

"I've never complained."

"Not in so many words, maybe."

"So, what do you want, Jack? You want me to not see anyone, so you don't have to worry about me?"

"Hell, no! I want you to be happy, Mom. You deserve that more than anyone I know. I just know you. You think you can keep it light and keep it fun, and when you say that, guys hear something else. I don't want to see anyone take advantage of you. I won't let them."

She laughed. "And you think I would? I'm not stupid, Jack. And I'm sure as hell not naïve."

"I know. I'm sorry. I should shut up and butt out. I mean, it's Seymour Davenport. How long is he even here for? It can't be for long. If you want to see him while he's here, you go ahead."

"I will, thank you very much. And he's here for ten days." She couldn't resist adding, "Though he's already talking about what we might do after that."

"He is?"

"Yes."

"When can I meet him?"

"We've been on one date, Jack."

"And when are you seeing him again?"

"This afternoon, and no, you can't come and meet him."

He smiled. "That's okay. I need to get back to work anyway. But if you're going to keep seeing him after he leaves town, I want you to introduce me to him before he goes."

"And if I don't?" She arched an eyebrow at him in a challenge, but he took the wind out of her sails with his reply.

"Then I'll know that what I think doesn't matter to you, and I'll accept that."

"Aww, Jacky." She reached across the table and squeezed his arm. "You know that's not true."

He gave her a wicked grin. "I sure do, but I got you, didn't I? And now I know that I'll get to meet him."

"Only if I'm going to keep seeing him."

"And we both already know that you are."

~ ~ ~

Seymour brought the SUV to a stop outside Chris's house and cut the engine. He'd forgotten how much he enjoyed driving. It wasn't far from the resort up here, but it was as far as he'd driven in months.

He reached over to the passenger seat and picked up the flowers he'd bought in town and the little bag he'd brought from the cabin. He checked himself out in the rearview mirror and then chuckled. He was like a kid—excited to be driving by himself and nervous about his date.

He got out and locked the door before making his way up the path to Chris's front door and ringing the bell.

She opened it with a smile. "Hey. You're early."

It took him a moment to make his voice work. She looked beautiful. There were dozens of beautiful women in his everyday life; women who worked for him, the wives of his colleagues—and their friends. They always seemed to bring along a friend—a beautiful, single, available friend. They never managed to capture his interest. He could appreciate the beauty, but he rarely felt any attraction, and certainly no connection. They didn't make him feel anything at all—except, usually, bored after the first ten minutes of inane conversation. Chris was different from them; just standing there on her doorstep, wearing blue jeans, a multicolored shirt, and a smile, she made him feel. He felt the attraction, he felt the connection, and even more than that, she made him feel ... his mind searched for the word and then shut down when he found it. She made him feel hope. He and Kate had named their daughter Hope for a reason.

"Hey," he answered. "I'm sorry. I ..."

She waved a hand at him. "No sorries. I told you, I'm the same. It's nice to know that I can expect you early. Usually, the only person I make plans with is my sister, and she's always late. Come on in."

He followed her through to the kitchen. He liked her house. It was small, but it was bright and neat. It had a good feel to the place—it felt like Chris.

He held out the flowers, feeling foolish. He should have given them to her straight away. "I brought you these."

She took them with a smile. "Thank you. I was starting to wonder if you were going to just carry them around with you as a prop."

It took him a moment, but then he laughed. "You're not going to cut me any slack, are you?"

"I can if you need it ...?" She raised an eyebrow.

"No. I don't. I'm a bit rusty at this whole thing."

She took the flowers and pulled a vase from a cabinet. "You don't date much?" she asked as she filled the vase with water.

He let his gaze rest on her backside as she bent to get the vase and then busied herself at the sink. "I haven't. Not much." Did he want to tell her that it had been a couple of years since he'd been on a date—or that even then it had only been to appease an old friend? He'd dated some over the years since Kate died, but he hadn't been able to make himself care. He'd just gone through the motions. A couple of the women had developed feelings for him—or, at least, they'd claimed to. He'd found it hard to believe since he'd felt nothing in return. After that pattern had repeated itself a few times, he'd stopped making himself even try. "Do you?" He wasn't sure if he should ask—wasn't sure if he wanted to know the answer. She talked about keeping this light and fun. Maybe it was a form of entertainment to her—a way to pass an evening here and there that held no meaning for her.

She turned to face him and leaned back against the sink. "I've dated some. A couple of guys since I've been here at the lake."

"How long have you been here?" he asked too quickly; he knew it.

She laughed. "I've been here a few years now. It's hard to believe that the time's gone by so fast. Don't worry; I'm not some man-eater. But I am a social creature."

He nodded. "I don't mean to pry. It's none of my business."

"It's not prying. I don't mind telling you. We're getting to know each other here, right? These are the kinds of things we need to know if we're going to be friends."

Friends. Was that how she was seeing this? Was she making a new friend? Would he be okay with that if she were? He would. He could see her being a good friend—except for one small detail: he wanted her to be more than that.

She raised an eyebrow at him. "Did I say something wrong?"

"No. Forgive me. I'm overthinking here."

"Want to share?"

He shook his head. "Probably not. I think it's better to go with your philosophy of just seeing where this goes and having fun. I could derail us by wanting to talk and ask questions and figure things out. But perhaps none of it will matter, so we're better off just enjoying our time. Do you want to go straight to the beach?"

"Sure." For a moment, he wondered if she wanted to talk more, but she smiled. "Let me get my purse and we'll go."

She gave him a puzzled look when he opened the car door for her. "No Ivan today?"

He smiled. "No. You gave me a wake-up call last night. I sent him a message this morning and told him to take the day off. I even got the car rental place to drop a car off outside his cabin so he can go and explore if he wants to."

He went around to the driver's side and was surprised when he buckled himself in, and she leaned over and pecked his cheek. "That was sweet of you. I'm sure he'll appreciate that."

He did. Seymour had felt bad. He'd admitted to Chris last night that he wore blinders when it came to his work. He hadn't realized that those blinders were narrowing down Ivan's options in life just as much as his own. He didn't want to do that to the kid and planned to treat him better in the future.

Chapter Six

When they reached the beach, Seymour slung his arm around Chris's shoulders as they walked down to the water. She smiled up at him, happy to see him relaxed.

"When was the last time you walked on a beach?" she asked.

"Last night."

She laughed. "I mean before that."

"Not for a long time."

"I thought as much. Though to be fair, there aren't many beaches in Montana."

"No."

"That's where you live, isn't it?"

He shrugged. "I spend a lot of time there now. Since Hope moved there and got married."

"And the rest of the time?" Now that she thought about it, he mustn't spend all his time in Montana. She didn't know much about the stock market, but she figured he'd need to be in New York sometimes or wherever else that kind of business took place.

"I move around a lot. I suppose the house in Malibu is the one I've thought of as home the most."

"And you don't walk on the beach there?"

"No." He smiled. "I don't make the time to do things like that. I do spend time staring out the window at the ocean sometimes—if that counts for anything."

"It gives me some hope for you. Though I have to say, it seems like a waste to me. Why would you live there if you don't make the most of the beach?"

He shrugged again. "It's beautiful. It's ..."

She could tell he was really thinking about the question, as if it had never occurred to him before. After a few moments, he looked down at her. "I don't know how this is going to sound to you. I don't think I've ever considered it before, but I live there because ... well, because it's a suitable address for someone like me."

She laughed. "You mean it's where the rich people live?"

He nodded. "Yeah. I do. I haven't thought of it that way until now, but that's the reason."

"Why do you look like that? I think it's perfectly normal. We all tend to go where our people are—where we feel comfortable. I live here because my kids are here."

"I know, but it's just dawning on me that since I left Montana—since Kate died—I've lived in places that seemed suitable. Not because I wanted to, just because I had to go somewhere."

Chris thought she understood. "Believe me, if I could have left Texas under my own steam, I would have. I would have gone anywhere."

He nodded, looking lost in his thoughts.

"But now you're back in Montana when you can be." She smiled, hoping to make him do the same. "You want to be near Hope and Chance and little Dylan.

"That's right."

"And what about your work—can you do that from anywhere?"

"Mostly."

Chris looked up at him, wondering if she'd lost him to whatever thoughts or memories were plaguing him. "You know, I only started this because I couldn't believe that you live by such a wonderful beach and don't make the time to walk on it. I'm sorry if I brought up things you don't want to talk about."

He stopped walking and looked down into her eyes. "I'm sorry. You do make me question myself, but I see that as a good thing. I just need to learn to save my questions for later and think about them on my own time—not spoil our time."

"You're not spoiling anything."

His eyes twinkled as he smiled. "I'm not exactly being much fun, am I?"

She couldn't resist reaching up to peck his lips. "You're being real with me ... that's more important."

He closed his arms around her waist and kissed her before resting his chin on top of her head. "I told you that you'd keep me on my toes. Having fun and being real is new territory for me."

She rested her cheek against his chest. "I don't think they're new; it's just a while since you've visited them. It might do you good."

"You're good for me."

She closed her eyes and just enjoyed the feel of him. He was good for her, too, but she didn't need to tell him so.

~ ~ ~

Seymour tightened his arms around her, wondering if he should have said that. She was good for him, but maybe saying so would only confirm her suggestion that she could be a catalyst for him. That wasn't what he wanted. Perhaps he was thinking too literally, but to his mind, a catalyst got used up in the process of transforming something else. He didn't want to use her and leave her behind when he left. That thought made him smile.

He took hold of her shoulders and leaned back to look into her eyes. "Since you're so keen for me to walk on the beach, why don't you come with me?"

She cocked her head to one side. "I thought that's what we're doing." She looked around. "This is a beach. Here we are." She smiled. "We might not be walking right now, but ..."

He laughed. "I mean on the beach by the ocean ... in Malibu. Come visit me when I go back?"

Her smile faded. "I thought we were playing this by ear. Taking one day at time?"

"We are. But I already know that I'll want to see you again after next weekend." He took a gamble. He didn't think there was much risk, but he needed to know. "Are you telling me you don't feel the same?"

She pursed her lips and thought about it for a moment. "I already told you, I don't play games. Yes, I'd like to keep seeing you after you leave."

He dropped a kiss on her lips and took hold of her hand and started walking again. "Good. Then you should come to Malibu."

"Okay, I will."

After their walk, Seymour drove back to the resort. He was glad that he'd given Ivan the day off. For one thing, the kid deserved a break. For another, he was enjoying this time alone with Chris. It wouldn't be the same if Ivan were chauffeuring them around.

He looked over at her. "Do you want to get a drink?"

"Sure. As long as you're prepared to bump into everyone I know—and no doubt face an inquisition."

He chuckled. "I can handle it if you can? Hope told me that we're the source of a thousand rumors already. You're the one who lives here and has to face the gossip."

"It doesn't bother me in the slightest." She winked at him. "I don't mind being talked about as the one who managed to snag herself a sexy out-of-towner."

He found an empty spot at the far end of the square and cut the engine before turning and reaching over to squeeze her hand. "Well, I don't mind being talked about as the out-of-towner who managed to get himself a date with Summer Lake's most beautiful woman."

She laughed. "Flattery will get you a long way with me—but not everywhere. There are a lot of beautiful women around here. I wouldn't claim to be the most beautiful. Not even close."

He squeezed her hand. "It doesn't matter what you claim or what you believe. Beauty is in the eye of the beholder. And this beholder is telling you, you're beautiful, Chris."

He leaned toward her, hoping she understood that he meant it. They weren't just words. She was beautiful, inside and out.

She held his gaze as she came closer, resting her arms on the center console. He cupped her cheek in his palm and stopped when their lips were no more than an inch apart. "Beautiful," he murmured, before closing the final gap.

Just like when he'd kissed her last night, he moved in, intending something slow and gentle but was taken over by a deep desire for her. He ran his tongue over her bottom lip and drew a little sigh from her that lit a fire in his blood. He sank his fingers in her hair, and her hands came up to cup his face as she kissed him back.

She made him feel like a kid again. He wished the console was gone so he could hold her close. Crazy thoughts flashed into his mind—thoughts of them driving away from here, away from the square and the people and continuing their kissing in the back seat. He shifted, his pants suddenly feeling too tight. He kissed her deeply, and she kissed him back, making it plain that she was feeling the same way.

Her breath was coming deep and slow when they finally came up for air. Her hand shook a little as she pushed her hair back from her face. "Phew!" She gave him a wry smile.

He nodded. "That's what I thought."

"I might need you to stop doing that."

His heart skipped a beat. She didn't want him to keep kissing her?

She laughed. "Don't get me wrong. It's not that I don't like it. It's just that, so far, we've only kissed where it's safe to do so."

He raised an eyebrow, not understanding.

There was a hint of color in her cheeks when she explained. "I'm not sure I'll be responsible for my actions if you kiss me like that behind closed doors."

His heart raced. He was surprised, but very pleasantly so, that she'd say it so plainly. "Do you think we need to stick with outdoor and public dates for a while then?"

He couldn't help but feel disappointed when she dropped her gaze and nodded. "I think we probably should." His heart rate picked right back up, and he could feel the blood rush to his temples when she looked back up and smiled. "We should, but I'm not sure I want to."

He hugged her as close as he could over the console. "I'm with you. I know we should." He dropped a kiss on top of her head. Just feeling her this close reinforced for him how much he didn't want to wait. He'd love to drive her back to his cabin right now and find out where their kisses led when the doors were closed. But he didn't want to spoil things between them by going too far too fast. He knew, just knew, that when they went there, it would be good—it would be fun. But he also knew that he was hoping for more than fun with her.

She surprised him when she sat up. "I guess we just have to treat it the same as everything else."

"Play it by ear?"

She nodded, and the way she smiled told him that they wouldn't be waiting very long.

He nodded. "Okay, but I think we should go in and have a drink now."

She gave him a mock pout. "And here was I thinking you were going to say we should go and find some closed doors."

He had to laugh. "You have no idea how hard it is for me not to say that."

He closed his eyes and sucked in a deep breath when she reached across the console and touched the front of his pants.

"I had an idea it would be hard."

He threw his head back and laughed. "It's very, very hard, and you are a wicked woman. Do you know this?"

She nodded happily. "Now that we've got it out in the open, I should warn you that I intend to be very wicked indeed until I can persuade you …"

He planted a kiss on her lips. "I'm persuaded. Don't doubt it. I'm trying to be a gentleman here."

She shrugged. "We're old enough and wise enough. We don't need to impose some artificial waiting period."

"No, but it's not totally artificial, either. I told you, I'm old school in some ways. We don't have to wait forever, but I don't want to rush in only to find that it makes you want to rush out."

She touched his cheek. "I know what I want, Seymour."

He jerked his head away at the sight of someone approaching the SUV. He thought he recognized the guy but couldn't place him.

Chris followed his gaze and groaned. "This is Jack, my eldest. Be warned. You're about to be interrogated."

He winked at her. "So, I shouldn't tell him my intentions?"

She chuckled. "No, but if they're anything like mine, I want to hear all about them later."

He didn't get a chance to reply as she let herself out before Jack reached them. He hurried out to join them.

"Mom." Jack leaned down to kiss her cheek.

"Jack, this is Seymour. I believe the two of you have met?"

Jack nodded and shook Seymour's hand. "We have. It's good to see you." He smiled and sounded pleasant enough, but Seymour sensed an undercurrent. He couldn't blame the kid. Seymour would feel the same way in his shoes.

"It's good to see you, too, Jack. And I have to say, I'm impressed. Hope took me over to the development at Four Mile Creek this morning. It's quite a project."

"Thanks. It's our best work yet." He smiled at Chris. "And my favorite project since it led to us all living here."

"It's a great place. I can see why you love it."

"It's a bit different than what you're used to, though, right?"

Seymour nodded. He knew Jack was testing him. He didn't mind. He was glad he was looking out for his mom. "It is. Your mom and I were just talking about how different it is from Montana or Malibu."

"And you're just here on vacation?"

"This time, I am. I came with Hope and Chance because they wanted me to take a break from work. I get too locked in sometimes." He turned to Chris. "I wouldn't mind getting a place here, though."

Chris's eyes widened. He knew she hadn't been expecting him to say that. He hadn't considered it himself until that moment. But Jack wanted to know what his intentions were, and in order to answer, he had to figure it out for himself. Hope and Chance spent quite a bit of time here. He had friends here in Graham and Anne. He wanted to see what could develop between him and Chris—so why not get a place here?

It seemed his answer was enough to satisfy Jack. He smiled and nodded. "Summer Lake seems to have that effect on people. It sneaks in and finds a place in your heart, and then before you know it, it has a hold on you and won't let go. Anyway, I won't keep you." He turned to Chris. "I wondered if you're free on Saturday night."

Seymour didn't miss the look she shot at Jack before she answered.

"Do you want me to babysit?"

"No!" Jack turned and grinned at him. "I wondered if the two of you might want to come out with everyone. "Isabel's going for a sleepover at Gramps's, and the whole gang is coming out for dinner and to listen to the band, it's been a while since we've all gotten together, and with Chance and Hope being here, you know Emma wouldn't miss it."

Seymour didn't understand the way Chris laughed at that. She turned to him. "Would you like to?"

"I'd love to."

"Great. I'll see you both then, if not before." With that, Jack turned on his heel and walked away.

~ ~ ~

Chris turned to Seymour and shook her head. "Sorry about that."

"Don't be. Do you want to go in?"

She nodded and took hold of his hand and started walking to the restaurant.

He gave her an inquiring look and held their joined hands up between them.

She laughed. "I don't mind anyone seeing or knowing if you don't."

"I don't mind at all—especially now that it seems I have Jack's approval."

"Like I said, sorry about that. He tends to be overprotective."

"And like I said, there's no need to apologize. I respect it. I thought I'd be in for a harder time than that from him. I have to confess that Chance did warn me."

Chris laughed. "Isn't it strange that the kids are looking out for us? It doesn't seem so long ago that it was the other way around."

He nodded but didn't smile.

"Something wrong?"

He gave her a sad smile. "I'm afraid I wasn't that great with Hope when she was growing up. I wasn't really there for her in the way I should have been. After ... after Kate."

Chris squeezed his hand. "I'm sure you did the best you could."

"It wasn't enough."

She could tell there was a whole lot of pain behind that statement. She sensed guilt, and she hated that for him. She knew how it felt—maybe not for the same reasons, but still, she knew how much it hurt to feel like you'd failed your children. "It seems like the two of you have found your way back to each other now."

"She found her way back through my walls." He smiled. "I can't take any of the credit. It was all Hope."

"I'm sure you did what you could."

He opened his mouth, seemingly to argue but changed his mind. They'd reached the door, and he opened it for her. "What would you like?"

"That depends. Are you planning to get me tipsy?" If he wanted to change the subject, she wasn't going to push him.

He chuckled. "I was hoping you'd choose and make that decision for me."

"In case ..." She made her way to the bar. "Hi, Kenzie. Can you make me one of your special margaritas?"

Chapter Seven

Seymour parked the SUV alongside the cabin and climbed out with a smile. It had been a great afternoon. He and Chris had sat out on the deck of the Boathouse and talked about all kinds of things. He was amazed at how quickly time flew by whenever he was with her.

He'd been a little tense about what they might do afterward. When she'd asked if he planned to get her tipsy, he'd considered it—but only for a moment. It seemed inevitable that their relationship would become a physical one at some point in the not too distant future. He didn't like to think that either of them would need any Dutch courage to take that step.

She'd made him laugh when she offered him a sip of her margarita. Apparently, Kenzie's *special* version was a virgin one—alcohol free, just like the beer he'd ordered in lieu of his usual bourbon.

He'd dropped her off at home afterward. He didn't want to go in with her. He wanted to be alone and digest what was developing between them. He liked it. He was eager to see where it might take them, but he didn't see any reason to rush it.

She'd felt the same way. She'd leaned across and landed a peck on his lips when he pulled up outside her house. Then she'd smiled. "You know I want to kiss you."

He'd nodded. "You know I want to kiss you, too, but we both know why we're not going to."

"Yet," she'd added.

He was glad they were on the same page.

He'd told her not to forget the bag he'd left on the kitchen counter for her earlier. It was the cookies he'd promised her. It was a silly gesture, he knew, but she'd put a word to the way he felt about his baking—it was allowing himself to be vulnerable. In his mind, giving her the cookies symbolized his willingness to be vulnerable with her, too. It didn't come easily or naturally to him, but it felt right to try. He was too good at putting up walls and hiding in his work.

Speaking of which … he checked his watch as he let himself into the cabin. He could get a few hours in this evening if he …

He turned around at the sound of a knock on the door and went back to open it.

Hope stood there, smiling at him. "You were in a world of your own there, weren't you? I called to you when you got out of the car, but you didn't see or hear me."

"I'm sorry, Hopey."

She laughed. "Don't be. It's nice to see you relaxed. You're usually on high alert, observing everyone and everything around you. I'm glad being here suits you—or is it something or someone else that's got you so relaxed and spaced out?"

He pursed his lips. Allowing himself to be vulnerable with Chris was one thing—telling his daughter all about it was another.

She slapped his arm. "Go on, admit it. It's Chris, isn't it?"

He gave her a rueful smile. "Yes. It is."

"That's wonderful, Dad. Everyone says she's an amazing lady."

"She is. But who's everyone? And have we been a topic of conversation?"

"Of course, you have. You knew that coming here. Chance warned you. This is small town life; that's the way it goes. And besides, Chris is like everyone's favorite aunt. They all want to see her happy, and I know it probably hasn't occurred to you, but you're a teeny bit famous, very good-looking for a guy your age, and considered quite a catch."

He stuck his nose in the air and tried to look offended. "For a guy my age?"

She laughed. "You know what I mean. I'm your daughter. I'm trying not to get weirded out that my sister-in-law's mother-in-law has the hots for my dad!"

He had to laugh with her. "I can see your point there. That doesn't sound too great, does it? It sounds like we should all be on some daytime TV show."

"No, it doesn't. It's just that I've only ever seen you as my dad, you know? So now it's weird for me. I like that you're spending time with Chris. I hope things go well for you, whatever that's going to look like, but it's strange hearing all the girls—and I mean the girls my age going all starry eyed and swoony over you."

Seymour chuckled at that. "Girls your age?"

Hope slapped his arm again, harder this time. "Yes, but don't even think about it. I'm doing well encouraging you and Chris, I couldn't even—"

He shook his head rapidly. "Neither could I, so don't even think about it. This isn't about me showing an interest in women all of a sudden. It's about me showing an interest in Chris in particular."

"I know, and I love it. Do I get to meet her?"

He thought about it.

"Whenever you're ready. I know you've only seen each other a couple of times."

"It's not that I don't want you to. I met her son today."

"Jack?" Hope looked wary. "I hope he wasn't too ..."

Seymour laughed. "I like it. He made it clear that no one messes with his mother, but I respect him for that. In fact, are you and Chance going to the Boathouse on Saturday night?"

"Yes, we are. I was going to ask if you want to watch Dylan. Frank and Alice were going to. You know they like to get all the time they can with him when we're here, but Alice's sister is coming to town for the weekend."

Seymour hesitated. He loved it when he got Dylan to himself for an evening when Hope and Chance went out, but he'd been asking about Saturday night because Jack had invited him and Chris to join everyone. But no. Dylan was his grandson. He couldn't pass up an opportunity to have him for an evening. "I'd love to."

"Great, thanks. You know what Chance is like. He doesn't always want to go out with the whole gang, but this time he's looking forward to it."

He smiled. "Of course. You know I love having him."

"And what are you up to this evening?"

"I think I'm going to get some work done."

She gave him a stern look.

"Come on, Hopey. I've hardly opened my laptop since we arrived. I've been out for dinner with old friends. I've had two dates with Chris. You can't tell me I'm overdoing it."

"No, I don't suppose I can. We're going to eat at the restaurant. Do you want me to bring you something back?"

"Yes, please. It'll save me cooking."

"Anything in particular?"

"Whatever looks good and you think might survive the ride back here."

She laughed. "I'll see what I can do."

She made her way back to the door, and he followed. She reached up to peck his cheek before she left. "I'm glad you came, Dad."

"So am I, Hope."

She let herself out and stopped halfway down the steps and turned back. "I am such an idiot! Forget about Saturday night, would you? You're going to want to see Chris! What was I thinking?"

He smiled. "You were thinking that I'd want to have my grandson for the evening—and you were right."

"No! I'm not going to take away your chance for a Saturday night out with your new lady."

He frowned. "She's not my new lady. At least, not yet. And if she is going to be, then she'll have to understand that my daughter and my grandson are important to me."

"I know we're important to you. But this is about timing— you can see us any time you like."

"True. But if Chris is going to be my lady then there's no reason that I can't see her any time we like either, is there?

Don't argue, Hope. You offered me an evening with my grandson. You're not going to take it away from me now."

Her lips pressed together into a thin line. It was a mannerism that she'd picked up from her husband. On Chance, it could appear quite menacing. On Hope, at least to Seymour, it just looked comical. He laughed. "Even Chance can't intimidate me with that look—you don't stand a chance. Go get your dinner and don't forget to bring me something back."

She blew out a big sigh and made her way down the steps. "If you're going to insist on giving up your Saturday night, then I'm going to do something to make it up to you."

"There's no need."

"There is for me. And besides, it'll be a surprise. So, you can't argue about it."

He smiled as he watched her walk down the path back to the cabin where she and Chance and Dylan were staying. She stopped before she rounded the corner and waved at him. "Love you, Dad."

He raised his hand. "Love you, Hopey."

He stood there for a long time after she'd gone. Just a few short years ago, he'd barely seen her from one year to the next. He'd checked out of life after Kate died when Hope was twelve. He'd shut down and closed out his friends and family. Unfortunately, he'd closed Hope out, too. He hadn't known how to cope. He hadn't wanted to deal with life or with people. He hadn't been able to console himself and had no clue how to console his daughter. She was a resilient soul— strong and independent—though whether those were natural traits that had seen her through the years after her mother's death, or whether she'd developed them in order to survive that period, he still wasn't sure. All he was sure of was that he'd abandoned her when she needed him the most.

He'd tried to manage her life without truly being a part of it. She'd stayed with her aunt and uncle—his brother Johnny and his wife—whenever she could. They had three boys, her cousins. They were better able to supply her emotional needs than he'd been. He couldn't even handle his own.

He blew out a sigh. She'd once told him that she wished he cared as much about being close to her as he did about being in charge of her. It hurt so much because it was true. He couldn't bear to allow himself to be close to her. He'd tried to orchestrate her life so that she was cared for and provided for—and so that he didn't have to look into her eyes every day. Her eyes were the same as her mothers, and every time he looked into them, he saw his own pain mirrored there. He'd failed them both.

He gave himself a shake and went back inside. All of that was behind them now. Hope was her mother's daughter. She had a big heart, and she'd forgiven him for all his mistakes. She'd been much kinder to him than he'd been to himself.

He closed the door behind him and went to sit at the dining room table, where he opened up his laptop.

It was strange how things worked out. He and Hope had grown close when she met Chance. And Seymour's initial intention had been to run Chance out of her life.

Now, because of Chance, they were here in Summer Lake, and it seemed to Seymour that his life was about to move into a new chapter—if he was ready to let it.

He pulled his wallet out of his back pocket and took out Kate's picture. She smiled back at him—so beautiful, so young. She'd been gone such a long time. He smiled at her. "You can stop looking at me like that now. You told me before you went that I had to find someone new. I told you it'd take a long time and someone very special. I wasn't wrong, Kate, but I think I might be there now."

~ ~ ~

Chris sat down at the kitchen counter and pulled the bag toward her. She couldn't help smiling as she opened it and saw the cookies. Who would have thought that the formidable Seymour Davenport was a secret cookie baker? She went and poured herself a glass of milk to go with them.

She groaned when she bit into one. It was wonderful. That didn't surprise her. He was one of those men who seemed to be good at everything he did. Baking cookies might be outside his comfort zone, but she couldn't imagine him screwing it up.

She pulled her phone out of her purse and took a photo of them with the glass of milk beside them and sent it to him.

I knew I was in for a treat tonight. Thank you.

She smiled when his reply came almost instantly

You're most welcome. But you know that wasn't the treat I had in mind.

She laughed. It wasn't what she'd had in mind either, but she was kind of glad it had worked out this way. If he'd come back here with her, they would have gone to bed together, and their friendship would have changed. It wasn't that she didn't want to go to bed with him or for their friendship to take the next step, but she was enjoying the anticipation. They were getting to know each other better first. In her experience, once sex was part of the equation, things changed. Men tended to fall into two camps, the first kind stuck around while the sex was new and exciting, then drifted away after a while, dates and phone calls becoming fewer and further between. The second kind was scarier; she thought of them as the needy ones. Once you had sex with a needy guy, they wanted to spend more and more time with you and started to treat you like their mom. Maybe in their minds, that was how relationships worked—old school, traditional gender role relationships, that was. Chris wanted nothing to do with that kind of thing. She was a free agent and a free spirit. She valued her independence, and she valued a strong, independent man. She had no intention of trading cooking and cleaning for financial support—or anything else, for that matter.

That was her one hesitation with Seymour. He'd admitted a few times to being old school in his views. Granted, he hadn't shown any kind of sexism or even shown that he was a traditionalist when it came to gender roles, but still. In everything else, he seemed almost too good to be true. So, it wouldn't surprise her if, once they slept together, he transformed into a needy guy. That would be a shame, but she was a practical soul, and she knew it was a distinct possibility.

She tapped out a message. That was why she planned to enjoy this initial phase of their friendship as much as she could—just in case it came to a crashing halt once things got physical.

It wasn't what I had in mind either. But I can make do. For now.

She wondered how he'd respond to that. She didn't have to wait long to find out.

I don't think I'm going to be able to make you wait too much longer.

She smiled.

Good. I don't want to.

You don't?

Yes and no.

Why no?

Because it might spoil things.

That's what I'm afraid of too.

You're afraid?

Honestly? Yes.

Why?

Because right now, I feel so hopeful. Everything is possible. If we screw it up, then that hope dies.

You'd rather live in hope and never know?

Not never.

For a little bit longer then.

A little bit. How about you?

I've been thinking the same thing. When we take that step, everything changes. It either gets even better, or it all falls apart.

We could be cowards and never cross that line, so we never find out.

What, just live in anticipation and never …?

Forget I said that. Never isn't an option.

Phew!

He didn't reply to that, and she waited, wondering if this conversation had been a bad idea. Maybe they shouldn't be talking about it all in advance. Maybe it'd be better to stick with her usual MO of playing it by ear. She couldn't help feeling that this was right. She liked that they each felt comfortable enough to talk about it. She didn't want to talk so much that they took the magic away, but this made her feel closer to him. They were figuring it out together, not staying in their own heads and trying to figure it out from there.

She jumped when the phone rang in her hand, and she smiled when she saw his name on the display.

"Hey."

"Hey. I wanted to hear your voice."

She laughed. "Do you want me to talk dirty to you?"

He laughed with her. "That's okay. I can wait on that, too."

"You might be waiting a very long time. That's not a talent of mine."

He was quiet for a moment. A shiver ran down her spine when he spoke again. "I can teach you if you like."

"Ooh! Yes, please! Wait, are you joking with me?"

He laughed. "I guess you'll just have to wait and see, won't you?"

She chuckled. "You're making the waiting option sound less and less appealing all the time."

"Maybe I'm just teasing."

"If you are, you're very good at it. Though you might regret it on Saturday night." He didn't reply, but she could tell straight away that she'd said something wrong. "What?"

"I can't go on Saturday night. Hope asked me to watch Dylan. I'm sorry."

"Oh, my goodness, don't be sorry. Evenings with grandbabies come before anything else. I understand that completely."

"Thank you. Since that was going to be our next date, I called to ask what else you'd like to do and when. Maybe tomorrow?"

She smiled. "I'll be finished at the center at three."

"Do you want to do something then or wait until the evening?"

"I don't want to wait if you don't. You can meet me in the bakery just after three if you want. Did you bring your hiking boots?"

"I did."

"Good. You should wear them. And don't worry about Ivan; I'll drive."

"Okay."

"Okay. I'm going to go finish my cookies now. I'll see you tomorrow."

"Goodnight, Chris."

"Goodnight."

Chapter Eight

"Call me if you need anything, won't you?" said Hope.

Seymour smiled at Chance. "You'd think that she'd trust me with him by now, wouldn't you?"

Chance laughed. "I'm not entirely sure she trusts me with him." He hugged his son close to his chest and then nuzzled his face into his belly, making him laugh and wave his arms.

Hope pursed her lips. "Of course, I trust you. I just question your wisdom in getting him all wound up like that before you hand him over to Dad."

Chance grinned at Seymour and handed Dylan over. He wrapped his little fingers around Seymour's nose and giggled.

"We're fine, see?" said Seymour. "He's investigating my nose, then, when you two finally get out of here and leave us in peace, we're going to play with the blocks."

"I know you're fine with him, really. I suppose I'm just feeling guilty that I messed up your night out with Chris."

"You didn't mess up anything. We've seen each other plenty. We've been hiking, been out for dinner and for coffee, walked on the beach. And we've got the whole week left before I leave. She even suggested we should go four-wheeler riding—though I'm not sure if she was joking about that."

Chance laughed. "My money says she's serious. Chris knows how to have fun; she's always up for anything."

Seymour smiled at Hope. "So, you can relax. You might be doing me a favor giving me a night in to rest."

"Didn't she want to come over?"

He frowned. "It didn't occur to me to ask her. I love watching Dylan but I wouldn't have thought it'd sound like a fun date."

"Oh, I thought you'd asked, and she didn't want to." Hope gave Chance a look that Seymour didn't understand.

"What?"

"Nothing."

"No, tell me. That look you just gave Chance says I screwed up somehow, but I have no idea how. I thought I was being considerate, not asking if she wanted to give up her Saturday night to spend it in domestic mayhem with junior and me."

Chance raised an eyebrow at him. "I'm no expert at this kind of thing, but my guess would be that Chris might have liked that."

Seymour stared at him. "You think?"

Hope laughed. "I do. This way it seems that you're happy to share dates and fun times with her, but you're not inviting her into your real life."

He frowned. "That's not true. I ..." He shook his head. "I suppose it could seem that way."

"Don't sweat it," said Chance. "I don't think it's that big of a deal." He looked at Hope. "Is it?"

"No. Sorry. It's just me thinking too much into it."

Seymour nodded, but he felt a little deflated. "Jack had asked her if she wanted to go out and see everyone. I wasn't going to ask her to give that up."

Hope smiled at him. "No, you're right. Ignore me."

Dylan had grown bored with all the talking and tugged on Seymour's ear, making him smile. "What do you want, grandson?" He giggled and then got a very determined look on his face as if he were concentrating hard. A moment later, Seymour smelled what he'd been concentrating on. He made a face at Hope. "I'll have to ignore you. This little guy needs a fresh diaper."

Hope held her arms out for him. "I'll change him before we go."

Dylan leaned away from her and snuggled against Seymour's chest, making his heart buzz with happiness.

"That's okay. You two get going. We can handle this, can't we?"

Dylan smiled up at him and gripped the collar of his T-shirt, as if to say, *I'm sticking with you, Granddad.*

Hope laughed. "Okay, fair enough. But call me if you need anything. We can always come back early and trade out with you so you can get some time with Chris later."

He waved at hand at her. "I told you, it's not a problem."

Dylan grabbed hold of his fingers and gummed on his knuckle, making him laugh. "You two can stand around here as long as you like, but we have a diaper to take care of." He picked up the changing bag and slung it over his shoulder before carrying Dylan through to the living room where he laid out the mat on the floor.

"See you later."

He glanced over his shoulder and smiled as Chance took Hope's hand and they let themselves out.

Chris pulled up a seat at the bar and looked around. Of course, she was early, but she was even earlier than usual this evening. She was a little disappointed that Seymour wasn't going to be here, but they'd spent plenty of time together in the last few days, and they had plans for the rest of the week, too.

She was a little surprised at herself that he'd filled her thoughts while she was getting ready, and that she wasn't as happy about this evening as she usually was on a Saturday night when all her friends and family were coming out.

"Hello, stranger."

She smiled when she saw Clay's security guy, Adam, standing beside her.

"Hey, you! How's tricks? I haven't seen you in a while."

Adam shrugged. "I've been around. From what I hear, you've been busy."

"What do you hear?" she asked with a smile.

"That you've been spending time with Seymour Davenport."

"I have. He's a good guy."

"I believe so. Good for you."

"Thanks. I should introduce you to his driver, Ivan. He's here by himself, and since Seymour's been driving us around himself, I reckon Ivan will be at a loose end."

Adam smiled. "I already met him. He's a good guy. In fact, he's coming out tonight. I'm off, since Davin's keeping an eye on Clay and Marianne, so I said I'd hang out with Ivan for a drink."

"Oh, that's good. I don't like to think of him all by himself with nothing to do."

Adam laughed. "You worry too much. You don't need to take care of everyone, you know."

She shrugged. "I don't. I don't interfere, I just—"

"It wasn't a criticism. You looked out for Davin and me when we first came here, too, and we appreciate it. This line of work can leave you with a lot of time on your hands in a place you don't know. It's sweet of you to look out for us. All I'm saying is don't get so busy looking out for everyone else that you forget to have fun yourself. Where's Seymour? Don't tell me you're early and he's late?"

She laughed. "No. He's never late. He's as punctual as I am. He's not coming this evening."

Adam frowned. "Why not?"

"He's watching his grandson while Chance and Hope come out."

"I see."

"Don't look like that. I see it as a good thing. I like him better for wanting time with his grandson than I would if he gave that up to spend an evening with me."

"I can see that. As long as you're okay. Marianne and Clay should be here any minute. Are you going to hang out with them?"

"Them and everyone else who comes. You know me, I'm a bit of a butterfly. I like to flit around and check in with everyone."

"Yeah. I've always admired that about you. My mom won't go anywhere unless my dad or one of her friends goes with her. You're not like that."

"I'm not."

"Look, here's Dan."

She smiled when she saw her younger son come into the bar and look around. She waved to catch his attention, and he made his way over to them with a smile on his face. "Hey, Mom, Adam."

Adam nodded. "Good to see you, Dan. I'll find you later. I have a couple questions for you about the new security system we're running at the house."

Dan smiled. "Okay. I don't know much about the systems you use."

"Yeah, but if anyone can figure it out, you can." Adam turned back to Chris. "It's good to see you."

"You, too, Adam."

Once he'd gone, she smiled at Dan. "And how are you?"

"I'm good, thanks, Mom. I've been busy with work this last couple of weeks. I feel like I haven't seen you much."

"That's okay. What are you working on?"

"You know I can't say."

She laughed. "I do. It fascinates me. I want to know."

He shrugged. "It's all classified."

"I know. At least tell me how Ryan is? Is he going to come up to visit any time soon?"

"It's funny you should ask. We were talking about that the other day. He said he'll try to come in the next month or two."

"Oh, good. He'd a good boy."

Dan laughed. "He's hardly a boy."

"You're all boys to me, Danny. Just because you're all grown up now and have families of your own, it doesn't make any difference. Has Ryan found himself a girl yet?"

"No. I don't think he's even looking."

Chris made a face. "If he's not going to get over Leanne, he should get back together with her."

"They've been over for years, Mom. They can't even stand to say each other's names."

Chris laughed. "And that should tell you all you need to know, right there. If they were over each other, it wouldn't matter to them."

Dan shrugged. "You know I'm no good at any of that stuff. I'm just lucky that Miss keeps me on track." He gave her a sly smile. "What about you, though? How are things going with Seymour?"

"They're going well. He won't be here tonight, though. He's babysitting Dylan."

Dan nodded. "That's good."

She raised an eyebrow at him. "Good that he's not here? You don't like him for some reason?"

"No. Good that he's getting some time with his grandson. From what Chance said, he's a workaholic. They weren't sure if he'd stay the whole ten days here or if he'd leave to get back to work. I figured he was sticking around to hang out with you. Hearing that he's babysitting, too, gives me hope that he does know how to have a life outside of work."

Chris stared at him. "You always see things differently than the rest of us, don't you?"

Dan smiled. "I think differently. It's just the way I am. You know I want to see you happy. I think Seymour's a good guy. If you two are going to keep seeing each other, then it's nice to know that he has a life he can invite you to be a part of. I was concerned that he'd been working all the time and you might be a distraction he kept on the sidelines for when he needs a break."

"Wow. You've given this some thought, haven't you? More than I have."

"You're my mom. I need to know that you're okay."

She leaned in and gave him a hug. "Thanks, Danny."

They both turned when Marianne and Clay joined them. "Aww, isn't that sweet. Have you got one of those for your Auntie Marianne?"

Dan gave her a brief hug and then pointed to the patio where Missy was sitting with some friends. "It's good to see you, but I'd better get Miss's drink to her." He nodded at Clay and then moved farther down the bar.

Marianne grinned at Chris. "Sorry. I didn't mean to scare him off. It's just that Dan hugs are so rare, I had to get one while he was giving them out."

Chris laughed. "That's okay. I don't blame you one bit." She turned to Clay. "Good to see you."

"You, too." He bent down and kissed her cheek. "And where's Seymour? He's a good guy. I want to tell him what a catch he's landed himself."

She laughed. "He's not here tonight."

"Why? What could be more important than a night at the Boathouse with you?"

"A night in with his grandson."

"Ah." Clay smiled. "That's a tough one to compete with." He smiled at Marianne. "There's not much that could take me away from a babysitting date with little Penny."

Marianne raised an eyebrow at Chris. "And you didn't offer to help?"

Chris laughed. "You think I'm such a party animal that I chose to come out instead? No. He didn't ask, and it wasn't my place to offer. We've only seen each other a few times. Grandbaby time is sacred as far as I'm concerned."

"I suppose. Does that mean this is just a passing thing for you?"

"No." Chris knew that her sister was wondering if she saw Seymour as just a fling. It was a fair question; she wasn't one to get into anything serious with a guy. Whatever was going on between Seymour and her felt different, but she didn't want to get into how different—or even why. "We don't know what it is yet. And there's no rush to figure it out."

Clay smiled at her. "You don't want to talk about it? That's fair enough. But I know Seymour, and I know you. I have high hopes."

She shrugged. "We'll just have to wait and see."

~ ~ ~

It was almost midnight when Chris pushed open the doors of the bar and stepped out into the cool evening air.

Seymour smiled when he saw her. He was sitting on the low wall at the edge of the parking lot with Ivan and Adam.

Hope and Chance had come back to collect Dylan half an hour ago and—at their urging—he'd decided to walk up here and see if he didn't run into her. He'd been surprised to see Ivan sitting outside drinking a beer with Clay's security guy. Adam had encouraged him to go inside and find Chris, but he'd preferred to wait out here. He didn't want to intrude on her evening, and it felt good to sit and drink a beer with the guys. It wasn't something he got to do very often.

Adam punched his arm. "It's been great talking with you, but there she is. I hope you're not planning to let her walk home alone?"

Seymour frowned. "She wouldn't do that, would she?"

Adam laughed. "Yes, she would. This town is as safe as you can get, but I've tried to talk sense into her. She doesn't listen."

Seymour got to his feet. "I already know her better than to try and tell her what she should do. But I can at least walk with her." He smiled at them. "Wish me luck?"

"Good luck, boss," said Ivan.

Adam grinned at him. "You don't need it."

He strode across the parking lot to catch up with her. He'd thought that she was making her way to the line of taxis that stood waiting, but as Adam had predicted, she walked on by them.

"Chris," he called just before she turned the corner onto the side street that they'd walked down on their first date.

She turned and looked back. A huge smile lit up her face when she spotted him. "What are you doing here?"

He reached her and put his hands on her shoulders. "Oh, I was out for a late-night stroll and just happened to run into you by chance."

She smiled through pursed lips. "Is that true?"

"No. It's a big fat lie. The truth is that I've been sitting on the wall waiting for you to come out for the last half hour."

She laughed. "Really?"

"Yes, really. I hope you don't mind?"

"The only thing I mind is that you sat outside instead of coming in."

"I didn't want to intrude on your evening."

"I wish you had."

"I'm here now. Do you want to go back inside?"

"No. Things were wrapping up in there anyway. Do you want to walk me home?"

"You know I do." He slid his arm around her shoulders, and they started walking away from the square.

"How did your evening with Dylan go?"

He smiled. "We had a great time. We played with blocks. I read him a couple of stories. Dealt with a couple of diapers. It was fun."

"Isn't it great? I love the time I get to spend with Isabel. It's like having a little one all over again, except you get to give them back at the end of the day and get a good night's sleep."

He laughed. "That's true. I'm worn out after a couple of hours. I couldn't survive if I had to do that every day and didn't get to sleep through the night on top of it."

"That's why we have them when we're young."

"It is. And how was your evening?"

"It was good, thanks. Marianne and Clay were out. He sends his best. Asked if you'd like to catch up for a drink while you're in town."

"I would. If you like the idea?"

"Yes. It'd be fun. It'd be nice for me to see you with one of your friends, too. You're getting to see me in my home environment and with my people. I don't get to see you in everyday life."

"I wondered about that. Should I have invited you to join me and Dylan this evening?"

"No. That's your time. It's special. I wouldn't have wanted to intrude on it."

He smiled. "Is that the same as me not wanting to intrude on your night out?"

She smiled. "Probably. Would I have come? Yes. Would I have enjoyed it? Absolutely. Did I think it might be too much since we don't know what we're doing here? Definitely."

"So, it was exactly the same, then. That's how I felt about coming into the Boathouse when I got there."

She smiled up at him. "None of it's a big deal, though, is it? We're here now."

"We are. And we have the rest of the week before I have to leave."

She nodded.

"And the following weekend you're going to come to Malibu to see me, aren't you?"

Her eyes widened. "The following weekend?"

"I'd like you to."

She smiled. "Then I'll come."

Chapter Nine

Chris poured herself a cup of coffee and took it out onto the back patio. She liked to sit out here in the mornings. The back yard was peaceful. She wasn't much of a gardener, but the trees and flowering shrubs took care of themselves, so she had a leafy sanctuary and even a peek of the lake if she put her chair in the right spot.

Jack and Dan had wanted to buy her a house, but she'd put her foot down about that. They'd both done very well for themselves; she knew they could afford it, but that wasn't the point. They should spend their money on their own families, put it toward college for their kids—like she wished she'd been able to do for them. She didn't need a fancy place, and this house suited her just fine.

She leaned her elbows on the table and stared out at the lake. The sky was blue, the sun was warm on her shoulders. Life was good. Seymour was leaving tomorrow, but all good things came to an end. She knew that. They'd had a great time together. She was hopeful that tomorrow's goodbye wouldn't be a final goodbye, but even if it were, she'd enjoyed what they'd shared.

She took a sip of her coffee. They hadn't shared a bed yet. The right moment had never presented itself. They'd had fun joking about it; there was no tension. And, after all, they'd only had a week and half together. That was no time at all, in the grand scheme of things.

Tonight, they were going out for drinks with Marianne and Clay. A shiver ran down her spine as she wondered what they might do at the end of the evening. She hoped that things might naturally fall into place, but at the same time, she didn't want to force them into place just because this was his last night here.

She heard her phone ringing and made a face when she realized that she'd left it on the kitchen counter. She considered just letting it ring, but that wasn't in her nature. She hurried inside, hoping it might be Seymour. It was a number she didn't recognize.

"Hello?"

"Hello, Chris. This is Hope."

"Oh! Hello, Hope. Is everything okay?" Her mind raced. She hoped that Seymour was all right. Why would Hope call her otherwise?

"Yes. Everything's fine. I hope you don't mind me calling you."

"Not at all. What can I do for you?"

"I wondered if you'd like to meet me for coffee today—if you have time?"

"Of course. I have an appointment at the center this morning, but I should be done by eleven. You could meet me there. It's right by the bakery, in the same building."

"I know. That'd be great, if it works for you."

"It does. I have to confess that you've got me worried. Are you sure everything's okay?"

"Yes. Everything's great. I'm sorry, I didn't mean to worry you. It's just … well, I know you and Dad are enjoying each other's company. I've heard so much about you—from him and from everyone else. I thought that we'd run into each other while we're here, but we're leaving tomorrow, and … I just wanted to get to know you a little before we go. That probably sounds crazy."

Chris laughed. "If it does, then it's my kind of crazy. I've been hoping that we'd get to meet and talk properly, but since it hasn't worked out of its own accord, I'm glad you reached out to set it up."

"Thank you."

"No, thank you. I'll look forward to it. I'll see you just after eleven."

"Okay. I'll see you then."

~ ~ ~

Hope hung up, and Chance narrowed his eyes at her. "What are you doing, honey?"

She shrugged. "I want to meet her."

"You think that's wise?"

"Why wouldn't it be?"

"Because you should leave them to it."

"I'm not going to butt my nose in. I'm not trying to get involved in their relationship. I just want to get to know her. You all talk about how lovely she is and how much fun she is. I want to see that for myself. I just want to know who she is. I've never seen Dad like this. I'm happy for him, and I think it's great. I just …" She blew out a sigh. "Do you think I'm doing the wrong thing?"

"I understand."

She went to him and slid her arms around his waist. "I'm glad you understand, but that doesn't answer my question. Do you think I'm doing the wrong thing?"

He looked down into her eyes. "I wouldn't do it."

"But you're not going to tell me that I shouldn't?"

He pressed a kiss against her forehead. "You know damned well, I'm not. You've got to do what you think is right. And I'll support you in it. I just want you to know what you're doing. I'd kinda like to know what you're doing myself. What do you want to get out of meeting her now? Why can't you wait?"

She smiled. "I don't want to get anything out of it. I want to put something into it. The reason I can't wait is that we're leaving tomorrow. Dad says he wants to see her again. Wants to invite her to Malibu. But I know what he's like. You know what he's like. As soon as he gets back to work, he shuts the rest of the world out. I want to prepare Chris for that. I think he wants to stay in touch with her, but I'm afraid that he'll forget about her, just like he forgets about me. He doesn't mean to." She looked out of the window before looking back at Chance. "But just because he doesn't mean it, doesn't make it hurt any less when you're the one waiting for him to call."

Chance tightened his arms around her. He understood how much pain her dad had caused her while she was growing up. "Is this about Chris or about you?"

She tensed. "It's about trying to help Chris not feel as rejected as I did."

"And you think that's a good idea?"

She shrugged. "I don't know. I want to help them along if I can."

"It's up to you, honey. But I'd think long and hard about what you want to say. Chris is a grown woman. She can deal with however your dad acts in her own way."

Hope nodded. "Maybe you're right. Maybe I shouldn't say anything." She gave him a weak smile. "I can still meet her for coffee and get to know her."

"You sure can."

~ ~ ~

Chris sat by the window in the bakery watching the street. It was ridiculous, but she felt a little nervous about meeting Hope. It wasn't because of who she was—Chris had admired her as both a model and a designer long before she'd ever met Chance or come to the lake. She was concerned that, as Seymour's daughter, she might want to manage who got close to her father.

She smiled when she saw Hope walk in and look around. She struck Chris as a sweet hometown kind of girl—not the rich, famous heiress that she was.

"Hey." Hope came hurrying toward her and wrapped her in a hug. "This is weird, isn't it? I've been second guessing myself ever since I called you."

Chris laughed. "It is weird, but I'm glad you reached out. This way, we can get the weirdness out of the way and put it behind us."

"See? We think alike already. I hated the idea of us leaving here and me not knowing who you were or how you felt—or if you knew what to expect." She held Chris's gaze for a moment. "And if I'm honest, I hate leaving without knowing what Dad can expect."

Chris raised an eyebrow.

"Are you going to forget him once he leaves?"

Chris laughed. "No. I'm not. In fact, he's invited me to come visit him next weekend."

"Next weekend?" Hope looked shocked.

"That's how I reacted, too, when he first asked."

"But now you're okay with it?"

"Yes. I'm looking forward to it. What do you think of that?"

Hope smiled. "I think it's amazing. See, I wanted to warn you …" She frowned. "At least, I wondered if I should warn you that when he goes back to work, he tends to shut down. He closes everyone and everything out. But if he's already invited you to come visit …" Hope grinned. "I guess it's all good. I know I shouldn't interfere. But he's happy with you, and I want you guys to have a chance. I just want to do what I can to help you understand him—as much as I understand him."

Chris reached across the table and squeezed her arm. "Thanks, sweetheart—and you are a sweetheart. I wasn't sure why you wanted to see me, but you want the best for him, don't you?"

"I do. And I know that he can be hard to understand—hard to love. But he's worth it."

Chris had to swallow the lump in her throat. She squeezed Hope's arm a little harder. "He told me he didn't always get it right with you. But he tried. He did the best he could."

Hope's eyes widened. "He talked about it?"

"Only a little bit." Chris was concerned that Hope might not like her knowing about her history with her dad, but she needn't have worried.

Hope grinned. "If he's comfortable enough with you that he'll talk about that kind of thing already, then I'll shut up and butt out."

Chris laughed. "Don't do that."

Hope winked at her. "I couldn't, not completely. All I can say is that he's come a lot further than I realized. I still think of him as he was back then. But I should know better. He's come a long way this last couple of years."

"He still hurts."

"It's okay." Hope smiled. "You don't need to reassure me. I don't need him to cling to the past. I'm hoping with all my heart that he can step into the future. I'm not here to warn you off. I only wanted to try to help you understand him so that he doesn't scare you off."

Chris had to swallow again. "I hope he knows how lucky he is to have you as his daughter?"

Hope's eyes filled with tears. "I think he has some idea these days. For the longest time, he didn't know what to do with me. He didn't know how to love me, so he mostly avoided me. I guess I was worried that he might do that to you, too."

Chris's heart raced. Love was a strong word.

Hope smiled. "I'm not saying that you're there yet, or even that you'll get there. I just worry that you won't ever get there if you don't have some understanding of how he works—how far he's come."

"I'm not sure that we're even heading in that direction. I don't know if he'd want to, or even if I would. But I can tell you that he's a lucky man to have you for a daughter."

"Thank you. And for what it's worth, I'd be happy for you both if that's the direction you choose."

Seymour looked himself over in the mirror in the bathroom. He straightened his collar and smiled at himself. He felt more like himself in a dress shirt. He hoped Chris would like the look. He felt a little underdressed with no tie, but this was still a more formal look than he'd been used to here at the lake. Tonight was special. It was his last night here. He wasn't thinking of it as his last date with Chris, though. This wasn't the end. Just the end of their first chapter.

He was taking her over to the Lodge at Four Mile Creek for dinner. They'd eaten at the Boathouse and at Giuseppe's enough times that neither of them seemed special enough for tonight. He'd taken a ride over to the other side of the lake yesterday while she was working at the women's center. The restaurant there was more upscale. He hoped she liked it.

He turned at the sound of a tap on the door and went to see who it was.

Ivan stood outside, smiling at him.

"Is everything okay?"

"Everything's fine. I just wanted to check with you—you really don't want me to drive?"

Seymour smiled and shook his head. Ivan had been with him for a good few years now. He was a good man, a good employee—and after only a few days around Chris, he'd become a good friend.

"Come on in while I finish getting ready."

Ivan only hesitated slightly before he followed him inside. Before this visit to the lake, Seymour would never have asked him. He didn't even understand why. That was just the way things had always been. Now—thanks to Chris—they were different, and he liked it.

"Do you want a drink?"

"I'm good, thanks."

"Part of me wants to ask you to drive. Part of me wants to not share the drive home with you."

Ivan smiled. "I can see that. Part of me wants to tell you to let me so that you can have a drink. I can wear my earphones on the way back and listen to my music."

Seymour laughed. "I know you're not an eavesdropper, but it's not the same, you know?"

"I can't say I know. But I can imagine. I can't imagine … but then lots of people take a taxi home after a date."

"True. But it's not the same as being alone, just the two of us."

"I understand. I just wanted to offer my services one more time. I hope it's not out of line for me to say so, but I'm rooting for you."

Seymour grasped his shoulder. "Thanks, Ivan. What about you, though? You can take the night off. Have another night at the Boathouse. I'm guessing you made some friends here yourself?"

Ivan shrugged. "I'll probably take a walk up there if you don't need me."

"You should. I'm guessing you don't date much yourself, given how much you work."

"I don't need to. Mind if I ask you something?"

"What's that?"

"I heard there was a rumor that you might be buying a place here. Is there any truth to that?"

"Maybe. How would you feel about that? It'd just be adding one more house to the rotation."

Ivan smiled. "But I get the idea that if you do, we'd be spending a lot more time here than anywhere else."

"Perhaps. Why do you ask? Do you have an interest in spending more time here? Has someone caught your eye?"

"Maybe."

Seymour laughed. "I guess we'll have plenty of time to talk about it once we're back to the usual routine."

"I guess we will." Ivan checked his watch. "Sorry, but it's such a habit for me. You have seven minutes if you want to get out of here at your usual ten ahead of schedule."

Seymour chuckled. "Thanks."

"And final offer—do you want me to drive?"

Seymour shook his head. "Thanks, but no. I want the time alone with her more than I want a glass of bourbon."

He sat for a moment when he pulled up outside Chris's house. It amazed him how quickly this had all become familiar to him. He was driving himself. Pulling up in this quiet little street. He sucked in a deep breath and blew it out slowly. He was going to miss this. He was going to miss her. But no. He'd only have to miss her for a week, then she'd come to Malibu. And when she did, they'd make plans for whatever they wanted to happen next.

Chapter Ten

Seymour held Chris's hand as they walked through the lobby of the hotel. They'd arranged to meet Marianne and Clay in the bar for drinks before dinner.

"Hey, Mrs. Benson."

Chris smiled at the girl sitting behind the reception desk. "Hey, Roxy. How are you?"

"I'm good, thanks. Are you here for dinner?"

"We are, but we're having drinks first."

"Oh, okay." Roxy smiled at Seymour. "Nice to see you, Mr. Davenport."

Seymour smiled and nodded at her, and they carried on to the bar.

Chris raised an eyebrow at him. "Have you been here before? How do you know Roxy?"

He smiled through pursed lips. "Do you really want to know?"

She laughed. "Yes."

"Ivan and I came for a ride over here yesterday. I wanted to check the place out before I brought you. I wanted tonight to be special."

"Aww." She leaned her head against his shoulder. "Thank you."

He looked around when they entered the bar. "They're not here yet. Do you want to get a table, or would you rather sit at the bar?"

"I should have warned you. We'll have to wait at least twenty minutes before they arrive. It's a sister thing. I'm always ten minutes early, Marianne is always ten minutes late."

He laughed. "Then I suggest we get a table—unless you'd rather sit at the bar?"

"Yes, let's do that. I have to tell you, though, I usually sit at the bar and watch the world go by."

"We can do that if you'd rather?"

"No. I don't need to people-watch to entertain myself when I have you for company."

She led him to a table over the by the windows, and he pulled a chair out for her.

He looked thoughtful as he sat down.

"Penny for them?" she asked.

He shook his head. "It's nothing."

"Go on, tell me. Something has you puzzled."

He met her gaze for a moment. "I'm not sure I should tell you. I just had a reaction, and I'm trying to figure out how I feel about it. I don't know how you'll feel about it."

"About what?"

"Okay. You said you usually sit at the bar for twenty minutes while you wait for your sister. My reaction …? I didn't like that idea. I don't like to think of all the guys seeing a beautiful woman and trying their luck."

She laughed. "It's only me. Most of the guys around here are my sons' friends. I know everyone. Everyone knows me."

"I guess, but this is a resort town. I'm sure there are visitors passing through who'd love to get to know the beautiful woman sitting alone at the bar."

She nodded reluctantly. She wouldn't deny that it happened on occasion—or that she'd enjoyed some fun conversations that way. "I don't think it's anything out of the ordinary. I'd guess that scenario plays out in bars all over the world every night of the week."

"I'd have to agree with you." He gave her a resigned smile. "I'm sorry."

"What for?"

"For the fact that I don't like the idea of guys hitting on you when I'm not here to fend them off."

He looked so serious, she had to smile. "I'm a big girl, Seymour. I can fend them off all by myself."

"I didn't think for one second that you can't. I'm being a little more selfish than that. I don't want anyone hitting on my lady." Her heart raced as he held her gaze. His eyes were a deep green. "Is that wrong of me?"

"No. It's rather sweet of you."

"But …?"

She shook her head. "There's no but. I'm surprised you feel that way about me."

"Surprised?"

She nodded. "Your lady?"

He reached across and took hold of her hand. "I'd like you to be. If you want to? I'm surprised at myself, I suppose. I didn't think I'd feel this way this soon." He dropped his gaze then looked into her eyes again. "Am I making this difficult? Would you rather change the subject, forget I said that, keep this light and …?"

Chris drew in a deep breath and let it out slowly before she spoke. "No. It's scary, but I don't want to back away from it. I like the idea of being your lady—even if we don't know what that might look like. You don't need to worry about me going off with other guys I meet sitting at the bar, though. That's not my style."

"I didn't mean to imply—"

She squeezed his hand. "I know you didn't. I'm trying to reassure you, not chastise you."

"Thank you."

"So, if I were your lady, what would that look like?"

He smiled. "I think the first step is for you to come visit me next weekend. Come and see me in my life—instead of just on vacation—so that you know what you're letting yourself in for."

She laughed. "You make it sound like you might be a vampire who lives in an old creepy mansion."

He laughed with her. "I'm not quite that bad. But you should come. I want you to come and stay with me."

A wave of heat washed through her. "Stay *with* you?"

His eyes twinkled as he nodded. "That's what I'd like. But if that doesn't feel right, it's a big house—there's lots of room."

"I think I'd like to stay *with* you."

He leaned across and surprised her by landing a kiss on her lips. "I'd like that, too. And if you feel like you can put up with me after that, then I've been thinking about looking for a place of my own here."

"Your own house?"

He nodded.

"So, you want me to stay with you, but you don't want to stay with me?"

"I wouldn't invite myself."

She smiled. "Well, this is me inviting you. Unless my place isn't grand enough for you." She raised an eyebrow at him. She wasn't stupid. She knew he had more money than she could even imagine. But that wasn't the point. Money didn't mean much to her. Yes, it could make life comfortable—but she was comfortable enough just the way she was. If that wasn't enough for Seymour, then maybe they should figure that out now.

He laughed. "I love your place. It feels good; it feels like you. And since I'm coming here to be around you, there's nowhere else I'd rather be."

"Good answer."

He smiled, but she could tell that something was bothering him. "Go on, say it."

"It hasn't come up between us yet, but it'll have to at some point."

"What?"

"The whole money thing. If I'm honest, when I've dated in the past, there's always been a question in the back of my mind about whether they were only interested in my money."

Chris pursed her lips, but he held a hand up to stop her before she spoke.

"With you, I'm more concerned that you might reject me because of it."

That made her laugh. "I wouldn't reject you because of it. I admire that you're able to do so well for yourself. But I have to be honest. I'm not interested in what's in here." She tapped on his wallet which he'd set down on the table. "Only what's in here." She tapped her finger on the side of his head. "I'm interested in you for who you are, not for what you have."

He smiled and caught her hand, placing it over his heart where he covered it with his own. "I want to win you over with what's in here." His eyes burned a deep, intense green as he looked into hers, making her tummy flip over as shivers chased each other down her spine.

She nodded. "You already have."

Seymour felt as though his heart was buzzing in his chest. He hadn't been sure that he was winning her over at all—not beyond enjoying a short time together and flirting around the edges of a possible physical relationship. To hear her say that he already had, made him happy.

He came back down to earth when he saw Clay McAdam walk in. The woman by his side was unmistakably Chris's sister. A little taller, a little leaner, but the resemblance between them was hard to miss. Clay caught his eye and raised an eyebrow. Seymour knew that he'd have questions. He also knew that he'd wait to get him alone before he asked them.

"Here they are." Chris waved at them.

Seymour watched her hug her sister and Clay before he shook hands with them both. He'd met Marianne briefly that night in LA, but this felt like their first introduction. It was obvious that Clay was very much in love with her.

Once they were seated and the server had taken their order, Clay grinned at him. "It's good to see you. I'm glad you finally found your way up here."

Seymour smiled at Chris. "So am I. I can see why you like it so much here."

Clay laughed. "It's a beautiful place—with beautiful women."

Chris made a face at him. "You wouldn't know if every other woman in town were as ugly as sin. You've only had eyes for Marianne since the day you first came."

"You're right." He smiled at Marianne. "Can I tell them?"

Chris cocked her head to one side—telling Seymour that she was genuinely puzzled about what they might have to say. At first, he'd thought it was a deliberate move to indicate that she had a question, but in the time that he'd known her, he'd come to realize that it was an unconscious movement she made when she was trying to understand.

Marianne smiled at her. "I'll bet Chris can guess."

"Guess what?"

"That we finally set a date for the wedding."

Chris clapped her hands together happily. "That's wonderful! When?"

"The end of next month," said Clay. He turned to Seymour. "I hope you'll be able to come?"

"I wouldn't miss it."

"We're not exactly having a wedding party, but I imagine you wouldn't mind escorting the sister of the bride?"

He looked at Chris. "I'd love to—if she wants me."

She smiled at him. "I'd like that a lot."

"Good, that's settled then," said Marianne with a smile. "Now I know what I'm doing with the seating."

"Will you be back here in the meantime?" asked Clay.

Seymour looked at Chris. "I'll have to wait and see if I'm invited."

"You are. We just need to figure out when."

"And are you coming to the dinner?" Clay asked Chris.

As her head cocked to one side again, Seymour's heart sank. He hadn't invited Chris to the fundraiser dinner he was hosting in a couple of weeks. Not because he didn't want her there, only because of her insistence on playing things by ear.

Clay caught on and shot him an apologetic look. Marianne either didn't realize what was going on or was less forgiving. "Which dinner?"

Seymour smiled at her and then at Chris. "The one Chris doesn't know about yet, but that I'd like her to attend."

She didn't seem put out. "If you'd like me to attend, then you'll have to tell me when and where."

"It's a couple of weeks away. It's an annual fundraiser dinner that we host in LA."

She nodded. "What do you raise funds for?"

He hadn't told her about his charity work yet. He looked at Clay. He was the voice; Seymour preferred to work behind the scenes as much as possible and maximize the numbers.

"Don't tell me he hasn't told you about any of it?" Clay asked Chris.

"Nope." She smiled at him. "We've covered a lot of ground in a short time, but I'm sure there's lots we haven't told each other about yet."

"He's too modest. This guy," he punched Seymour's shoulder, "is the brains behind some of the biggest children's charities in the country. You know I've worked with Oscar for the last few years? Well, it was his Uncle Seymour who set that up. And even aside from the kids, he's probably raised more money for addiction recovery charities than any other person in the country."

Seymour didn't know what reaction he expected from Chris. He didn't like to make a big deal out of the charity work he did. It wasn't about how people saw him; it was about the contribution he could make. What he didn't expect was for

Chris to look so … so … he couldn't even put a word to the look on her face. Horrified was maybe too strong—maybe. Shocked was probably closer.

Marianne covered the awkward silence that ensued. "That's great. And here I was thinking that you were one of those men who was only interested in making the rich richer."

Her words might have sounded harsh, but she gave him an apologetic smile that told him she was just saying the first words that came into her head to give Chris a moment to pull herself together.

"A lot of people see me that way. And I don't make the effort to show them how they're wrong. I don't make money—for myself, my investors, or my charities—to impress anyone. I do it for how it feels to me."

He caught Chris's eye. "Of course, some people's opinions matter more than others."

She smiled. "I think it's amazing. I really do. I just had no idea that you were involved in addiction recovery work."

He chuckled. "If you talk to my daughter, she'd tell you that my involvement runs a lot deeper than fundraising."

Her smile disappeared again at that. Damn. He seemed to be screwing up every time he opened his mouth tonight.

Marianne got to her feet. "If you'll excuse me a moment?"

Chris got up and went with her to the ladies' room.

Seymour blew out a sigh and looked at Clay.

"Hell, I'm sorry. I didn't mean to throw a grenade in the conversation. I thought I was asking an innocent question about the dinner. I assumed you two would have talked about the fundraising."

"Nope. It never came up."

"You know why she reacted the way she did, don't you?"

"No again."

"Damn! I'm sorry. Her husband. He was an alcoholic."

Seymour nodded. She'd told him only that her husband had died young. "That's what killed him?"

Clay nodded. "And from what I understand, made her and the boys' lives hell before it did."

"Thanks for filling me in."

"I'm sorry. And this is your last night here?"

"Yes."

"Well, then, I think when they come back, Marianne and I will make our excuses. Give the two of you the evening to yourselves. It strikes me you have some talking to do."

"Thanks. She might prefer you to stay."

Clay chuckled. "Even I know Chris well enough to know that if she does, she'll say so."

Seymour had to smile. That was part of what he loved about her. She was straightforward, spoke her mind. His smile faded. That was also why it surprised him that she hadn't told him about her husband. Maybe it was simply that she didn't trust him well enough yet. You didn't share that kind of thing with casual acquaintances. He'd hoped she saw him as more than that.

When she and Marianne arrived back at the table, she was more composed. She even gave him an apologetic smile.

Clay patted her hand. "I was going to make up some BS excuse about getting a phone call and needing to leave, but I think we're beyond that kind of thing. We're all friends here. So, I'll just ask. Do you two want us to leave you to it? I'd guess you have some talking to do and you don't need us here for it."

Chris chuckled. "I love that you're as up front as I am."

Clay smiled. "I've found it saves a whole lot of time and heartache."

She turned to Seymour. "What do you think?"

He nodded. "I enjoy this guy's company, and it's been lovely to see you, Marianne, but I'm sure we'll have other opportunities. This is my last night. I'd like you to myself, and now it seems we have things to talk about."

"Okay." Chris smiled at her sister. "I'll call you tomorrow after he leaves, and you can take me out to console me."

Marianne and Clay laughed at that. Seymour couldn't hide a smile.

Chapter Eleven

Chris watched Marianne and Clay walk away. Even after they'd turned the corner, she continued to stare at the space where they'd been.

"Are you okay?"

She finally turned to look at Seymour and nodded. "I am. I'm sorry I reacted like that. I surprised myself."

"You certainly surprised me."

She chuckled. "I can imagine. There's Clay lauding all the good work you do, and I must have looked horrified."

"You did. Do you want to tell me why?"

She blew out a sigh and took a sip of her drink. "Want to? I'm not sure I do, no, but I should. I owe you that."

"You don't owe me anything. You tell me as much or as little as you want in your own time. If tonight isn't the time, then we can forget it, move on."

"Tonight is the time. It's come up for a reason. I'd hate for you to leave tomorrow wondering what I got so het up about." She shrugged. "It's not even a big deal. Not anymore. It's just that I know a lot about addiction." She shot a quick glance at him. "Not first-hand experience. The boys' father. He was an alcoholic."

"I'm sorry."

She shrugged again. "So am I. He was a good man. At least, he wanted to be. But he had his demons, and the only place he knew to escape from them was at the bottom of a bottle. He tried to quit. Several times. Those recovery programs, they can help some people."

Seymour squeezed her hand. "They can only help people who are ready for them."

She held his gaze for a moment. There was a darkness in his eyes she hadn't seen before.

"Sorry. Go on."

"There's not much to say. It's the age-old story. We met. We fell in love. We got married and had two baby boys. He tried to stay sober. He'd manage it for a time, but he'd always go back. The boys—Jack especially—learned to hate him."

"Hate is a strong word."

She nodded. "I know it is, and it's still the word I choose. Jack's a good boy. He knew the way we were living was wrong. But it was all he knew. He wanted his dad to love him; he did in his own way. But he was bitter. He took it out on me, and on them. He was always sorry. Always promising he'd get sober and stay sober, and I was young and stupid, and I wanted to believe him. I did believe that one day he'd come out the other side. I wouldn't have stuck with him if I didn't believe that."

"But he never did?"

She shook her head sadly. "His final fall off the wagon was fatal."

"I'm sorry."

She met his gaze. "It is what it is. I like to be bright and upbeat and look for the positives when I can, but I'm a realist at heart. It was for the best. If he hadn't drunk himself into a stupor that night, he would have done it another night, or maybe he would have gone on for years or decades. Even if he had, he wasn't living, he was existing—a tortured existence, at that. And ..." she swallowed, hard. Wondering if she was going to share with Seymour something that she'd never shared with another living soul. She was. "And it was for the best for the boys and for me, too. There, I said it."

Seymour edged closer to her and wrapped his arm around her shoulders, hugging her into his side. She swallowed again and tried to blink away the tears that filled her eyes.

His voice was so gentle when he spoke. "It's okay. Cry if you need to."

She looked up into his eyes. "I'm all cried out over him; that was almost twenty years ago. It's you that's making me cry now. You're making me feel safe and cared for in a way I've never known."

He dropped a kiss on her lips and hugged her closer to his side. "You are safe with me, Chris. And you are cared for. More than you know."

She sniffed and pulled a hanky out of her purse and dabbed her eyes. She smiled at him. "I'm going to ruin the moment now and blow my nose."

He chuckled and sat back. "You're not ruining anything. You're making it real. You told me I wasn't used to allowing myself to be vulnerable. It strikes me that it's not familiar territory for you either."

She smiled. "You're right. It's not. I'm more into putting a brave face on things and getting on with it."

"I know. I've already learned that about you. That's why this means so much." He brushed a strand of hair off her face. "Thank you for trusting me, for telling me."

"I would have told you at some point. It was just hearing that you were involved in that kind of work, it … I don't know. It caught me off guard. It struck me how different you are—that I married an addict, and here, all these years later, I'm …" She stopped herself short. What had she been about to say? *Falling in love with,* that's what she'd been about to say! She must be caught up in the moment. She smiled. "Now, I'm growing fond of a man who does so much good work to help end addiction."

There was that look in his eyes again. That darkness. She'd grown to love his eyes. She still couldn't decide whether to call them green or hazel—sometimes they were deep green, other times almost brown with green and gold flecks. Of all the colors she'd seen in them, she hadn't seen any darkness until tonight.

"Are you keeping secrets? You said your involvement runs deeper than just fundraising."

He shook his head. "No secrets. Well, maybe."

She let out a short laugh. "Well, it seems like tonight's the night to spill them. Want to tell me?"

He nodded slowly. "I do. Part of me would rather not. I'd rather leave the person I've been in the past in the past. But he's a part of me, so you should know about him."

Chris's chest tightened as she wondered what he was about to confess. She'd vowed to herself that she would never get involved with another alcoholic. And as far as she was concerned, even after twenty years sober, an alcoholic was still an alcoholic. "So, tell me."

"It's not the booze for me. It's work."

She cocked her head to one side. "What's work?"

"My addiction. I'm a recovering workaholic."

"Oh!" A huge wave of relief rushed through her, and she let out a little laugh.

He didn't laugh with her. "See, that's why it's so easy for me to let it slide, to say it's not really a secret. It's much more acceptable to be a workaholic, isn't it?"

Chris nodded. "I was afraid you were going to tell me something much worse. I don't know what. I mean, I hardly see you as a drug addict type."

He shook his head slowly. "There is no *better* or *worse*. Drug addiction, alcoholism, workaholism, they're just different faces of the same underlying issue. Addiction. I do so much for recovery programs because there's a stigma that seems unfair to me." He blew out a sigh. "Life can be tough no matter what your background or your path in life. It's a part of human nature that we seek to escape our pain and our fears.

"I think most people seek temporary solace until they're able to move forward. For some of us, we get stuck. We can't find a way to move past the pain or the fear, so we continue to avoid it—by escaping. It's my belief that we self-medicate by whatever means are familiar or available to us. Some people use drugs, some people throw themselves into their work, some people drink, some people read or play video games. The vehicle we use isn't always labeled as a drug—and therefore doesn't carry the same stigma, but to my mind, very few people could cast the first stone."

Chris stared at him for a long moment. "I never thought of it that way before."

He smiled. "I don't think many people ever do. But I wish more people would. It's easy to jump to judgment and condemnation. But it's not helpful."

"I know. Believe me, I know."

He tucked his fingers under her chin and looked deep into her eyes. "I told you I hurt Hope; I turned away from her and escaped into a world I could cope with. Just because for me that world is work, doesn't make me any better than someone who turns elsewhere."

"Did you ever beat her?"

He shook his head rapidly. "No."

"Well, then. I take your point that addiction can have many faces, but as a survivor of the damage it can do …"

"Your table is ready."

They both looked up at the host from the restaurant who'd come to get them

Chris smiled at Seymour as they got up. "I'm glad I told you. I'm glad you told me. I think we know what we need to. We can move on."

He took her hand as they followed the host. "I'd like that."

"Do you want to come in?" asked Chris when he brought the car to a halt outside her house.

It'd been a good evening. Sharing about each of their past experiences had brought them closer. They'd laughed over dinner and left the past where it belonged—behind them. He didn't want the night to end.

He turned to look at her. "Do you want me to?"

She waggled her eyebrows. "I was thinking of a nightcap since you didn't have a drink."

He smiled. "Ah, a nightcap."

She nodded.

"In that case, yes."

He followed her up the path to the front door. Once they were inside, she turned to look at him. "Bourbon?"

"That'd be great."

He took a seat at the kitchen counter and watched her pour their drinks. He'd done well to keep a lid on his physical attraction for her so far. Even tonight, he'd had it in mind that they should say goodbye when he dropped her off.

Now that he was here, though, he didn't want to leave before morning. He knew that once they kissed, his desire for her would be hard to argue with.

She set his drink on the counter in front of him with a smile. "Do you want to sit outside?"

He followed her out onto the little patio and took the seat she offered him.

"Can you really see yourself staying here with me?" she asked.

He chuckled. "I absolutely can—but you're asking about the future, and I'm thinking about tonight."

Her laugh sounded nervous. "I was. I was thinking about my not-so-large, not-so-fancy house."

He bit back a comment about his very hard … and stuck with her line of conversation instead. "I've already told you. I like your place. It has a good feel to it. It feels like you."

"And you don't mind that it's different from what you're used to?"

He patted his lap and held his arm out to her. "Come here, while I explain something to you?"

The moment she sat on his knee, he closed his eyes briefly and questioned the wisdom of his gesture. But he pulled himself together. What he had to say was important, and he wanted to feel close to her while he said it. "I told you that ever since I left Montana after Kate, I've lived wherever seemed appropriate. I have homes in the places where my people are—my people, being business associates. My family— my brother Johnny and his wife Jean, their home base is Montana. I couldn't stay there. Hope moved to LA when she started modeling. Other than them, my people are people I work with. I've never chosen to be somewhere because I wanted to be there, only because it was convenient and logical to be there.

"This is different, Chris. I want to be here. I want to be with you. All the material wealth I've accumulated—it's a side-effect for me, not a goal in itself. I wasn't joking when I said I'm a workaholic. I've dedicated all my time to my addiction. I'm fortunate that it produces a positive—money, and lots of it. But don't go believing that that's why I do it.

"I think we're all seeking happiness, and we get there by whatever means we can. I thought happiness was beyond my reach after Kate. I threw myself into what I knew—work. You were seeking happiness in the places you knew you could find it—in your family, and I'd guess from what I know of you, in your ability to help others." He stopped.

"I'm not sure this is making any sense. What I'm trying to say is that what I'm looking for is to be happy. The houses, the money—they don't make me happy. You do."

She looked down into his eyes and dropped a kiss on his lips. "You make me happy, too. I'm going to miss you."

His heart clenched in his chest as he realized how much he was going to miss her, too. For a crazy moment, he wanted to ask her to go with him. But he knew better. There was so much he had to catch up on when he got back. It wouldn't be fair to ask her to come and then leave her by herself most of the time while he worked.

He cupped her cheek in his hand. "I'm going to miss you. But only until next weekend. Will you come on Friday?"

"As long as I can find a flight."

He pursed his lips. "I'll come get you."

"You will?"

"Yep. That's something you're going to have to get used to. I told you. I have a pilot. I have a plane."

"I know. Jack and his partner Pete have a plane, too. I admit I didn't ever think I'd be someone who flew around in a private jet, but I have done." She smiled. "And I'll be more than happy to if it means we get more time together."

"Good. Then can I come pick you up on Friday afternoon?"

"You can." She slid her arms around his neck and dropped a kiss on his lips. "And can you wait until then?"

He frowned, not understanding the question.

She wriggled on his lap and the way his body reacted, he knew what she was talking about. "If that's what you want."

"It is. I thought that tonight would be the night, but it isn't."

"It's not?" He tried his best not to sound disappointed.

"No. I can't tell you why, because I don't know. Right up to the moment I invited you in, I thought I was inviting you to … you know. But now that you're here, after everything that we've talked about tonight, I just want to feel close to you."

He nodded and tightened his arms around her waist. "I do feel close to you. Closer than I've felt to anyone, since Kate."

She rested her head on his shoulder. "Do you still miss her?"

"I do. It's different now than it was in the early years, but yes, I still miss her." This felt strange. The women he'd dated in the past hadn't asked about Kate, and he wouldn't have wanted them to. With Chris, it was different. Kate was a part of who he was—and he wanted Chris to know all of him.

She had a faraway look in her eyes that he didn't understand. "Are you okay?"

She smiled. "I am. I'm sad for you—for what you lost. I'm sad for me—for what could have been so great but never was. But I'm happy, too. Life is a funny old thing, isn't it? It keeps moving forward and takes you places you would never have dreamed of going. It brings new people into your life." She planted a kiss on his forehead. "People you would never have dreamed of meeting."

He nodded. "I never dreamed I'd fall in love in again."

Her eyes widened as she looked down at him.

He smiled. "That's what's happening here, Chris. I'm not going to hide that from you. I hope it doesn't scare you away, but it's the truth. I'm falling in love with you."

Her eyes filled with tears, and for a moment, he wondered if he shouldn't have told her. Was it too much, too soon—or just not something she wanted to hear?

"I'm sorry."

"Don't be. I'm not. I was deliberately trying not to say it. I said life brings new people into your life—I meant people you would never have dreamed of falling in love with—I meant you. I didn't say it because I'm a coward. I'm glad you're not."

"I almost was a coward. I don't want to scare you away."

She tightened her arms around his neck. "You didn't. You reeled me right in."

He chuckled. "I have to warn you. I'm not looking to catch and release."

"I don't want you to."

She lowered her head, and he slid his fingers into her hair, pulling her down so he could kiss her. The now familiar wave of desire rushed through him, but he didn't act on it. He wanted to reassure her that he was in this for the long haul. They'd talked about falling in love with each other. At this point in life, he saw love as a multifaceted treasure. Yes, the physical connection was a large part of it, but there was so much more that they could share sitting here talking and kissing under the stars.

Chapter Twelve

Chris closed up the office in the women's center and wandered through to the bakery. It had been a long few days since Seymour had left. They'd spoken on the phone each night, but it wasn't the same. If he were still here, she'd be rushing out after her appointments either to meet him here or to go home and deal with the other details of her life before she got to see him later. Now, she felt a little aimless—and that wasn't like her.

April smiled at her from behind the counter in the bakery. "You look like you could use a pick-me-up. Are you after a donut, a coffee or both?"

Chris laughed. "I'll take both and call it lunch."

"How are you? Have you had a heavy morning?"

"Not particularly. I had a follow-up meeting with Abbie. It sounds as though Michael is going to offer her the job."

"That's great. I'm sure his patients will be pleased to see such a friendly face behind the desk. Mrs. Evans has always been efficient, but she's a bit scary, too."

"She is, though she seems a lot more mellow since she decided to retire. Maybe she'd just had enough and wanted out."

"I guess. I hope she'll be happier in retirement. And I hope Abbie gets the job and takes to it. She deserves a break after all her family's been through."

"She does. I wish she'd leave town, though."

April made a face. "Why?"

"Because that way she'd have a fresh start. Be able to create whatever life she wants without her past weighing her down. I thought you'd understand that. What bothers me most is that she's giving up her own life to take care of her mom. And there's no reason her mom couldn't stand on her own two feet and take care of herself."

"Wow. You're right. I hadn't thought of it like that, but you're right."

Chris shrugged. "Sorry, it bothers me, that's all."

"It shouldn't, you know; it's Abbie's choice."

"I know. And I'm supporting her in her choices."

April laughed. "But I'm sure you've made it clear that she has other options—options that you think are preferable."

"I have, but she doesn't want to hear about them."

"Then let her be."

"I am!"

They both turned at the sound of the bell ringing when the door opened. Marianne came in with a smile. "I thought I might find you here. Do you want to get some lunch?"

Chris smiled. "I'm just about to if you want to join me. I'm going with the healthy option—coffee and a donut."

Marianne rolled her eyes. "I'll join you, but I'll have a salad." She smiled at April. "And I'll take a lemonade with it, thanks."

"Sure. Go and take a seat, I'll bring everything over."

Chris sat down opposite Marianne and smiled. "Did you want me for anything in particular?"

"Just for lunch. I wanted to see how you're doing."

"I'm fine. How are you and Clay? How's the wedding planning coming along?"

"Great, thanks. He's doing most of it. And Laura and Autumn are helping. They're all so into that kind of thing and—as you know—I'm not."

"Good for you. It'd drive me nuts to have everyone else take over the planning if it were me, but that's just another one of our differences. Is there anything you want me to do, or is it all taken care of?"

Marianne's smile faded. "Should I have asked you to do more? You're not put out, are you, that the girls are helping, and I haven't asked you?"

Chris laughed. "Not in the least. I'd love to help if you want me, but I don't need to be involved if you've got it all covered."

"Thanks. I didn't think you'd want to get lumbered with all the work, but I want to share the fun part—the most important part—with you."

"Which part is that?"

"Dress shopping. You know me. Dresses have never been my thing, but I want to wear one. The girls would love to go, but I want it to be you. Do you remember …?"

Chris's eyes filled with tears. "Of course, I do."

"How old were we?"

"Ten and twelve, maybe? I don't know. But I've never forgotten." Their parents had taken them to a cousin's wedding. And they'd both fallen in love with the beautiful dress she'd worn. As they lay in bed that night, they'd talked about their own weddings and how they each would wear a beautiful dress like that. They'd made a pact that they'd go together to buy the dresses when it was time.

Reality had stepped in, and neither of them had had a big wedding. Chris had worn a suit to the courthouse, and Marianne had worn jeans for her ceremony held in a barn.

Marianne smiled at her. "I think this time around we should do it right. I want you to come with me and help me find a beautiful dress. And when it's your turn, I'll come with you."

"My turn?"

Marianne gave her a knowing smile. "Don't play the innocent with me. You're in love with him, aren't you?"

Chris opened her mouth to deny it, but she couldn't. Instead, tears pricked behind her eyes and a smile spread across her face. "I didn't expect to fall for him. I don't think I even wanted to. But damn, Marianne. He's a hard man to resist—and I wasn't able to."

"That's wonderful. I'm so happy for you. I didn't think you'd admit it to me."

She smiled. "Neither did I, but I can't hide it. He's amazing."

"And I'd guess he feels the same way about you?"

"He says he does."

"What, you don't believe him?"

"I do. But the test will come now that he's gone back to work."

"But you're going to see him this weekend, aren't you?"

"I am. It's not about how long we spend apart. It's about his work. It's been his whole life. I don't know if he'll be able to give it his all and still have anything left for me. This might sound crazy; you know that up until this point I've been happy to date around the edges of my life. I haven't wanted to let anyone into it completely. It's different with Seymour. If he wants to keep me on the edges of his life, then I'd rather walk away."

"That's not enough for you?"

"It could be. But it'd mean that he's still hiding—hiding from pain and loss. I wouldn't hold that against him, but I'm ready to move forward in life. If he's not ..." She shrugged. She didn't know how to put it into words, but she knew that if Seymour was still addicted to his work, she wouldn't be able to be with him. He was right; his addiction might not come in a bottle, but if he still needed to lose himself in it, she wasn't going to let herself come second place to it.

"For what it's worth, judging by the way he was when we were all out together last week, I'd guess he's serious about you."

Chris smiled. "He's told me as much. But he's lived his life the same way for many years now. Just because you want things to change, doesn't mean you can change them." She knew that all too well.

"Well, I'll be keeping my fingers crossed for you. Maybe we'll be shopping for your dress one of these days. But in the meantime, when do you plan to come back from your visit to Malibu?"

"He's coming to pick me up on Friday afternoon, and we said it's for the weekend, so I guess I'll be coming back Sunday night or Monday. When do you want to go dress hunting?"

"Clay's going to LA for some meetings on Monday. I wondered if you wanted to meet there?"

"Okay. I'll have to see how it works out. Let me talk to him? I don't know if he planned to bring me back here on Sunday or what. It's about an hour's drive from Malibu into the city, isn't it?"

"I guess. Maybe an hour and a half. I'm sure Ivan could bring you, even if Seymour has to work."

Chris smiled. "Can you imagine what Mom would think if she could hear us now? Talking about flying around in private jets and having drivers take us places?"

Marianne laughed. "She'd tell us to get over our dreaming and come back to the real world and do the dishes."

"It does feel more like dreaming than real life if I stop and think about it too hard. All those years scraping for every penny and now everything's so easy."

"See, dreams do come true. I know mine have."

"I never dreamed of a rich man coming along to sweep me off my feet. Just a kind man who wanted to walk through life beside me and have my back."

"Seymour is definitely all of that. You're not going to hold it against him that he just happens to be loaded, are you?"

She laughed. "No. It just makes me wary—almost as though it's a dream too far."

"I don't believe there is such a thing. What's that quote? If you can dream it, you can achieve it?"

Chris nodded. "Yeah. I suppose. But let's come back to here and now. What are you doing this afternoon? Do you want to come back to my place and we can look at dresses online? That way you'll have some idea of what you like before we go."

"Good idea. See, this is why I need you. That wouldn't have occurred to me."

"One of us has to have her feet on the ground."

Marianne made a face. "Just don't keep them planted there too firmly. Let Seymour sweep you off them if he wants to."

"I'll try."

~ ~ ~

Seymour ran down the steps in front of the office and crossed the sidewalk to where Ivan stood waiting beside the car. He opened the door, and Seymour slid into the back and immediately pulled his laptop out of his briefcase and got back to work. It'd been a long day, and it looked like it'd be a long night, too.

"Was it a good day?" asked Ivan.

Seymour frowned and looked up. It wasn't like Ivan to interrupt when he was working; he knew better. He nodded curtly and looked down at the screen again. He fired off an email. He needed to set up an early morning meeting with the analysts. Next, he needed to …

"Are you looking forward to the weekend?"

He looked up again. Irritated now, that Ivan hadn't taken the hint the first time. This time he didn't bother to respond before he got back to his work.

He didn't look up again until Ivan pulled into the driveway back at the house. Once he brought the car to a stop in the garage, Seymour got out and started toward the door that led into the kitchen.

"Do you want to hang out and drink a beer tonight?"

Seymour stopped in his tracks. The question was so far out of left field, it took him by surprise. He turned around slowly.

Ivan stood beside the car, twisting the keys in his hands. "This time last week, we were still in Summer Lake, and I remember sitting on the porch of my cabin drinking a beer with you. I enjoyed that. I think you did, too. I'm probably crossing the line here, but we've only been back here a few days and the Seymour Davenport I got to know last week is nowhere to be seen. I miss him. I liked that guy."

Seymour glared at him for a long moment.

Ivan shrugged. "Fire me if you want to. Now that I know what it's like to work for a relaxed Seymour, I don't want to work for the other one."

Seymour's lips twitched. He couldn't help it. They curled up into a smile. "Are you calling me an asshole?"

"Nope. I'm just saying you were a lot happier when you weren't working. You were a lot more pleasant to be around."

Seymour blew out a sigh and jerked his head toward the kitchen door. "Do you want to come in?"

"Sure."

Seymour let them in and went to check the oven. The housekeeper had left it on low to keep a casserole warm.

He turned back to look at Ivan. "I don't have beer, but there's soda in the fridge and whatever you like in the bar. Are you hungry?"

"How about you fix the food and I'll bring the beer?"

Ten minutes later they sat out on the terrace. Seymour smiled and took a swig of the beer that Ivan had brought from the guest house where he lived. It tasted good.

Ivan grinned at him. "I knew I was pushing my luck tonight, but I had to do it."

"Thanks. I'm glad you did. I've fallen back into my same old ways."

"Do you have to?"

"What do you mean?"

"I mean, does what you do have to take every ounce of your attention?"

Seymour thought about that. "It's demanding; that's why I chose it. The stakes are high. I can't afford a lapse of judgment. Mistakes in this game cost millions—and those millions belong to my investors, not to me."

Ivan took a bite of his bread roll and nodded. "So, it is all or nothing then?"

"You won't meet any part-time hedge fund managers."

Ivan nodded but didn't say anything. Instead, he ate and drank and stared out at the ocean for a while.

Eventually, Seymour grew impatient. "I thought you were leading somewhere with your line of questioning."

Ivan shrugged. "So did I, but your answers made it clear that there's nowhere to go."

"What do you mean?"

"I had high hopes for you and Miss Chris, but from what you've said, she's only going to be an occasional weekend visitor at best, right?"

Seymour frowned. "That's not what I want."

"But it's all you have time for. You said it yourself."

"I didn't say I don't have time for her. I …"

"I know it's not my place, but if you remember, on the flight back here last weekend, you asked me to let you know if you were falling back into your old ways. I've tried dropping subtle hints since Monday. You've been in too deep to even pick up on them. Tonight, I realized that this isn't about you falling back into your usual habits and working too hard. This is about what you value in life. Your work is high value—in a financial sense. I know that. But I really thought that last weekend was a turning point for you and that you were going to find some way to compromise. You're not, are you?"

"I want to."

"But you just told me it's not possible."

Seymour blew out a sigh. "I'm not used to being put on the spot like this."

Ivan smirked. "Especially not by an employee. But that's the trouble, Mr. Davenport. If you go making friends with the help, they want to help you. And I only know how to be real with you."

"If we're friends, then you'd better call me Seymour. And I never saw you as the help."

Ivan laughed. "You didn't mean to, maybe. But you never saw me as a person or a friend until Miss Chris made you stop and think."

Seymour nodded grudgingly. "You're right. I'm sorry."

"No need. I'm not trying to make you feel bad about how you've acted in the past. I'm trying to make you think about how you want to act in the future. Do you want to be the guy you were the last couple of weeks while you were at the lake? I've seen hints of him before when we're in Montana. But when you're working, the mighty Seymour Davenport comes back. I'm sure he's the best in the world at what he does. He can move mountains and make billions, but he's not a great guy to be around."

Seymour took a long swig of his beer. "You're right. I've been Seymour Davenport all this time because I didn't have anything else to be. Actually, that's not true. I could have been Hope's father or Johnny's brother or Oscar, TJ, and Reid's uncle. But being any of those things meant being here in the real world. And I didn't want to be here. I didn't want to be the broken father, brother, uncle who lost his wife and lost his way. I wanted to be the mighty Seymour Davenport, who could still make millions despite being broken. I knew how to do that."

"I get it. But it doesn't make you happy, does it?"

Seymour shook his head.

"That's the thing, Mr. D." Ivan winked at him. "I can make it less formal, but I can't bring myself to call you Seymour."

Seymour chuckled at that.

"The thing is that you don't get to be happy until you face reality. The brokenness, the pain, the loss, the fear—the whatever it is for you. It doesn't go away. You have to push on through it. Learn to live with it. You won't ever find happiness by avoiding reality. You can find a temporary high, but you always have to come back down from there, and when you do, all the sucky stuff is still there, still waiting for you to deal with it."

Seymour held his gaze for a long moment. "How did you get so smart?"

"When I got clean. I was lucky. I went into the program after just a couple of years. I was even luckier when I came out that you hired me. You know I can never repay you for that. But I think I can help you by sharing what I learned with you. You can't hide from pain. I know you've done it for a long time. And maybe you've hidden for so long that there's nothing left to be afraid of. It seems to me that when you let yourself live life, there's a lot you enjoy. I'd guess that you're ready to be happy again—but you're not going to find happiness at work."

"So, what are you suggesting?"

Ivan shrugged. "I don't know. You're the smart one, or at least you're supposed to be. I'm just like that little cricket on your shoulder. I'm not here to tell you the answers—just to remind you to ask yourself the right questions. What do you value: hiding or happiness? And if the answer is happiness, how do you find it? They say if you keep doing what you've always done, you'll keep getting what you've always got. To me, that says that if you want something different, you'll have to do something different—it's up to you what that something's going to be."

Seymour gave him a rueful smile. "It strikes me that you are the smart one. I'm lucky I have you around."

"Don't look too happy about it. I did the easy part. It's up to you to figure out what you want and how you're going to get it."

Seymour nodded and stared out at the ocean as he sipped his beer. He already knew what he wanted. What he had to figure out was how much he was prepared to change to get her.

Chapter Thirteen

Chris felt like a little kid waiting for Christmas as she stood watching out the windows for Seymour's jet to come in to land on Friday afternoon. It had been a long week since he left, and she was excited to see him again.

She smiled when she spotted the plane, just a gleam of silver in the sky at first, growing larger until it turned onto the final approach and came in for a smooth landing before taxiing toward the FBO building where she stood.

Her phone buzzed in her purse, and she pulled it out.

I just landed.

She smiled as she tapped out a reply.

I know. I'm here watching.

She saw the door open, and the pilot let down the steps. A few moments later, Seymour appeared at the top of them. Her tummy flipped over at the sight of him. He must have come straight from work. Instead of the jeans and T-shirts she'd grown used to seeing him wear, he was dressed in pants and a dress shirt. He'd probably been wearing a tie earlier, but it was gone, and the top button of the shirt was undone, giving her a sudden urge to unfasten the rest of them and finally run her hands over what was underneath.

She looked around guiltily, grateful that no one could hear her thoughts.

When she looked back out the window, he was striding across the tarmac. Her heart raced. He looked like something out of a movie. This didn't feel like real life—at least, not her life.

She hurried over to the doors to meet him. When he came through, he smiled, and her heart beat even faster. He came to her and closed his arms around her, lifting her off her feet and twirling her around before setting her down again and planting a kiss on her lips.

"I missed you, Chris."

She touched his cheek. "I missed you, too. Though if this is the greeting I get after just a week apart—"

He dropped another kiss on her lips. "Just a week? It seemed like forever to me. I've decided a week is the longest I can go without seeing your beautiful face." He tightened his arms around her waist. "Without having you this close to me."

She laughed. "So, absence did make the heart grow fonder?"

He took her hand and started walking her toward the doors. "My heart was already very fond of you. It took the absence—and a bit of tough love from Ivan—to help my mind catch up."

She looked up at him. "That sounds like you have a story to tell me."

He chuckled. "I do. Ivan's a good kid. Better even than I realized. What's important, though, is this week has made me realize how much I want this, Chris. I want you; I want there to be an us. We just need to figure out how we can make it happen."

She sucked in a deep breath. "Can we make it up as we go along?"

He wrapped his arm around her shoulders. "Of course, we can. I'm sorry. I didn't mean to come in like a freight train. I just need you to know. I'm all in. It's one thing to talk on the phone. It's different when we're together. When I can hold you and look into your eyes and tell you I love you."

He held the door open for her and let them out into the parking lot, leading her to a little grassy area with benches. When they reached it, he put his hands on her shoulders and looked down into her eyes. "I love you, Chris."

Her heart was racing. She'd been excited to see him; she'd known that their friendship would move to another level this weekend, but she hadn't expected this. "I love you, too. You crazy man!"

He laughed. "You think I'm crazy?"

"You're acting a little that way. I knew there was more to you than the stuffy, formal guy I saw on the financial TV shows, but I didn't know there was this side to you."

He surprised her by closing his arms around her waist and swinging her around again. "I didn't know this side of me still existed, but you bring it out in me. You make me happy."

"Well, can you make me happy and tell me why we're out walking in the parking lot when I thought we were getting on a plane?"

He laughed. "They need to refuel. I'm doing my best to loosen up here, but public displays of affection aren't really my thing. I didn't want to do this inside and have people watching."

He cupped her face between his hands and tilted her head back. A sigh escaped her lips as his eyes locked with hers; they were that beautiful deep green color. He lowered his head until his lips were less than an inch from hers. She closed the final gap, pulling him down to her.

Just like every time they'd kissed before, he made her knees weak. She sagged against him as he kissed her deeply. His strong arms held her up, close against his chest. She clung to him and kissed him back, their tongues mating, hands roving from hair to cheeks to shoulders to … ooh! She moaned as his hands closed around her butt and pulled her against him—hard. It seemed he was more than happy to see her. She sank her fingers in his hair and rocked against him, desire mounting inside her.

When they finally came up for air, he winked at her. "I think we should go and see if they're finished refueling. I need to get you home."

She shook her head.

His smile froze and then disappeared. "You don't want to go?"

She laughed. "Of course I do. But there's no way on earth they could have refueled in that short time, and I'd rather wait out here than inside where I can't kiss you anymore."

He laughed and pulled her back to him. "In that case …" He lowered his head and claimed her mouth again, and she got lost in the kiss.

~ ~ ~

Seymour took hold of her hand as the plane banked to the left, turning onto its final approach. She turned and smiled at him.

"I wasn't sure how this weekend was going to go. Wasn't sure how enthusiastic you'd be to see me again after a week back in your own world."

He smiled. "I have to be honest, the first few days I fell back into my old routine. I got lost in work. I didn't intend to. I wasn't seeking escape like I usually do. It just ..." He shrugged. "There's the element of habit, you know? Even when you don't need something anymore, don't crave what it can do for you, when it's all you know, it's what you do."

She nodded. "And you said Ivan helped you?"

He chuckled. "He did. I almost bit his head off, but he stood his ground. Even said I could fire him if I didn't like what he had to say. He was more concerned about me than he was about his job."

"Aww. He looks up to you so much. I'm glad he looks out for you, too."

"I'm grateful to him. You're at the bottom of it all, though. The way you treated him last week at the lake made me think about the way I treat him—and it wasn't good enough. I want to kick myself when I think that he's been with me all this time and I mostly ignored him—treated him more like a piece of furniture than a friend. He told me I saw him as the help. I denied it, but he's right. I don't want to be that way anymore, Chris."

She smiled. "You won't get a chance to be if you're going to keep spending time with me. I don't know what it's like to employ people—in any capacity. I only know to treat people as equals, and if I catch you doing anything other than that, I'll let you know about it."

"Thank you. I'm coming to see there are a few areas where I might need my butt kicking."

She laughed. "I can do that if that's what you want."

When the plane landed, he thanked the pilot, Jeff, and introduced him to Chris.

She shook his hand. "It's a pleasure to meet you, Jeff. Have you worked for him for long?"

Jeff flicked a glance at Seymour and looked away again. "Four years now."

"I hope he's good to you?"

Jeff nodded. "It's a great job."

Chris laughed. "Diplomatic answer, well done. Hopefully, sometime soon, you'll get to spend another weekend at Summer Lake."

Jeff nodded. "It's a great little town."

"It is, and there are a lot of good people there. I'll introduce you. I imagine in your line of work you end up spending a lot of time hanging around. It'd do you good to make some friends up there."

Seymour smiled at him. He didn't do well when he was put on the spot like this, but he promised himself that he'd make some time to have a chat with Jeff soon, maybe invite him up to the house. He smiled to himself. He could come and hang out and drink beer with Ivan and himself. "Your weekend is your own. Chris and I won't be flying anywhere."

"Okay."

Seymour met his gaze. "I mean, you're not on standby. Take a break, relax, have a few beers."

Jeff grinned at him. "You're sure?"

"Absolutely sure, and we need to start scheduling in more downtime for you. Call Karen in the office and ask her to set something up next week. Tell her we'll need an hour—or better yet, get her to book us a lunch."

"Okay."

Chris touched Jeff's arm. "Don't worry. You're not in trouble, and he's not losing it. He's just finally waking up to the fact that people are more important than work."

Jeff shot a glance at him, and he nodded. "She's right. I'm going to be making some changes, but I think you'll like them."

Chris took hold of his hand as they walked into the general aviation building. "I'm proud of you. I think you're going to have more fun if you decide to shake things up a bit."

"I know I am if you're going to shake it up with me."

She smiled up at him. "I'm all in."

Ivan was waiting outside and came around to open the car door when he saw them.

Seymour had to smile when Chris went to give him a hug. "It's good to see you again."

Ivan grinned at Seymour over her shoulder. "It's good to see you, too. I hope this is the first of many visits."

"I do, too. And you're sure you don't mind taking me into the city on Monday?"

"Mind? I'm looking forward to it."

"I'm not as excited about that," said Seymour. They both turned to look at him. "Only because Monday will mean that the weekend is over, and we haven't even started it yet."

Ivan gestured to the car. "Then let's get going. Your chariot awaits."

~ ~ ~

When the car pulled up in front of the gates, Chris did her best to look nonchalant. She'd been expecting a big house, but this place was something else. The gates swung open, and Ivan pulled forward along the driveway that seemed to be at least a mile long.

He brought the car to a stop in front of the steps—not just steps up to a front door, but a grand sweeping stairway that reminded Chris of something out of a movie.

Ivan got out to open her door, and Seymour came around to meet her.

"You have yourselves a great weekend," said Ivan. "You know where I am if you need me."

"Thanks," said Chris. "You, too. Oh, wait. I need my bag."

"Don't worry, I'll—" began Ivan.

Seymour smiled at him. "That's okay. I'll get it."

Chris got the idea that it was out of the ordinary for Seymour to follow Ivan to the trunk of the car and take the bag from him but decided not to ask about it.

They watched Ivan pull away. "Where does he live?"

"In the guest house by the pool."

She laughed. "Of course, he does."

Seymour made a face at her. "It's not that unusual."

"Not around here, I suppose. I'm sorry. I don't mean to be … I don't know how I'm being. It's just that this …" She swept her arm out in a gesture that took in the grand house and the amazing ocean view. "It's not what I'm used to."

He took her arm, and they walked up the steps. "I know, and as I've said before, I hope you won't hold it against me."

She laughed. "I'd be crazy if I did. It's lovely. It's just, it makes me wonder what's important to you."

He opened the front door and led her inside. "Do you want a drink?"

She nodded and followed him through the spacious hallway to a beautiful den with a bar that ran along one wall.

"What would you like?"

She laughed as she eyed all the bottles. "Whatever you want to make me."

"Wine?"

"That'd be good."

"This?" He handed her a bottle of Cab Franc that looked very familiar.

She smiled. "Yes, please. Where did you find that?"

He smiled. "Chance introduced me to it. It's very good; it's not one of the big labels, but apparently, it's a very good winery."

"It is. The boy who owns it is a friend of Jack's, Antonio."

He smiled. "It's a small world."

"It is."

He poured their drinks and came to sit down beside her. "I wasn't avoiding your question."

"Did I ask one?"

"Not directly, but you said that all of this makes you wonder what's important to me. It's a fair question. It'd be fair to assume, judging by the house and the plane and the lifestyle, that material things are most important to me. Especially when you add in the fact that by the way I've treated them, you wouldn't guess that people are important to me—but they are. I want to reassure you, Chris. I'm better than the man I've been. I didn't chase wealth because I craved it. I chased wealth because it was easier for me to attain than any genuine human connection was. I knew how to trade, I knew how to analyze the markets, I got results—big, tangible results in the form of large sums of money.

"On the other hand, with the people who were left in my life, all I produced was sadness and disappointment. I let my daughter down when she needed me the most. I didn't know how to be there for her. I couldn't stand to be around my brother and his wonderful wife. I love them dearly, but all I could see was what I no longer had."

He shook his head. "I know I sound like an asshole. I'm not trying to justify my choices, only to explain them to you so that you don't see me as materialistic and heartless. It's not that I don't have a heart; it's just that it was too battered and bruised for me to use it."

She leaned her head against his shoulder. "I would never think of you as an asshole." She turned and smiled up at him. "You've done the best you could. I guess what I want to know, is why you think you're ready to change it now?"

"Because of you."

She pursed her lips.

"I'm not saying that being with you has brought this sudden miraculous change to every aspect of my life. Things have been changing for a few years. It started when Hope met Chance. I had to change, and I discovered that I wanted to. Chance taught me a lot about people. Since then, I've worked my way back into my life. Spent more time with Johnny and Jean and their boys. I don't know. Hope made me see that my work was an addiction, and I've been doing my best to break it. You've come along at the right time. You're like the capstone. You've drawn together and strengthened everything that I've been learning and waking up to." He squeezed her hand. "You're good for me."

She reached up and kissed his lips. "I want to be."

Chapter Fourteen

After dinner, Seymour took Chris's hand and led her out onto the terrace by the pool. Seeing the way she looked around her made him realize that he rarely came out here. He looked around, too, taking in the beautiful view of the sun setting over the ocean.

She looked up at him. "You really are crazy if you don't ever walk on that beach. It's amazing."

"Do you want to go down there?"

She nodded eagerly, making him laugh.

"Okay."

When they reached the bottom of the steps, she kicked off her shoes and wriggled her toes in the sand. "That feels so good." She looked at him and raised an eyebrow. "Don't tell me you're going to leave yours on?"

"No." He removed his shoes and socks and wished that he was wearing shorts. That way, he wouldn't have the question of whether to roll up his pant legs or not.

Chris chuckled as she watched him. "Roll them up. It might make you look like a goofball, but it beats them getting wet and sandy."

He gave her a rueful smile. "Thanks for the tip."

They walked down to the water's edge, and Chris dipped her toes in. "Oh, that's not as warm as I thought it would be."

Seymour followed her and sucked in a deep breath as a wavelet washed over his ankles. "It's freezing!"

She laughed. "You should know this! You should come for a walk down here every morning before you go to work. I can't believe you live here and you don't make the most of every minute. If I lived here, I'd start every day with a walk on the beach and at least dipping my toes in."

She looked so beautiful, the last rays of the sun touching her skin with gold and the wind whipping her hair around her face. She was so alive, so in the moment. He wanted to capture this moment and bottle it. "You should stay here, and we'll make that our morning routine."

She shook her head. "I can visit here sometimes and make that my routine, but you need to figure out your own."

He chuckled. "You don't want to share yours with me?"

"It's not that. You need to find your own. I can distract you from your usual routines, but you won't break them until you make new ones. Walking on the beach, freezing your toes in the ocean—they're not things that you'd do. You need to find something that feels good to you."

"You're right."

She came to him and slid her arms around his waist. "I'm not saying I don't want to share with you. I'm only saying that if you want to change, it has to come from within."

He dropped a kiss on her forehead. "I understand. Don't worry. I'm not looking to you to be my savior."

"Good. I can't be. You have to save yourself. We all do."

He slid his arm around her shoulders, and they walked on along the shoreline. "What do you want to do this weekend?"

"I just want to hang out with you. I could spend hours down here on the beach. Or I could relax by the pool ..." She turned to look up at him. "When was the last time you swam in that pool?"

He smiled through pursed lips. "Not for a while."

She pushed at his arm. "I bet it's been years, hasn't it? Why do you even have a pool if you don't use it?"

"It hasn't been years. It's only a few months. I got in with Hope and Dylan a few months ago."

She laughed. "That doesn't count. I mean, for your own enjoyment."

"I enjoyed that. And just because I don't use it much, Ivan does. He often swims early in the morning before we leave for the office."

"Well, that's something, I suppose."

"How about tomorrow we just hang out here, then? We can walk and swim and whatever else you want to do."

She surprised him when she stopped walking and slid her arms up around his neck. "There is something else I want to do, but I don't want to wait until tomorrow before we do it."

His arms closed around her waist and held her against him. She was so soft and warm, her full breasts felt so good pressed against his chest. She held his gaze as he lowered his head to hers. He knew what she wanted, and he didn't want to wait until tomorrow either.

She pulled his head down to kiss her, and when their lips met, that now-familiar urgency coursed through his veins. His hands moved of their own accord. One came up to cup the back of her head, holding her in place as he explored her mouth with his tongue. The other hand slid down and closed around her rounded ass, kneading and squeezing, eliciting little moans from her that only intensified his need for her.

She broke away from the kiss, and her eyes shone as she looked up at him. "I don't want to wait anymore, Seymour."

He took her hand, and they walked back up the beach to the steps that led to the house.

~ ~ ~

He stopped in the kitchen and put his hands on her shoulders. "Are you sure?"

She chuckled. "I'm sure I'm sure. Are you?"

He nodded. "I've been sure a few times already, but the moment always changed before we saw it through. I started to wonder if maybe you're not so attracted to me that way."

She shook her head slowly. "You really are a crazy man, Seymour. Look at you." She ran her fingers over his biceps, and a shiver ran down her spine. You're gorgeous; there's never been any question that I was attracted to you physically. You're a very attractive man. I didn't want to go there too soon because it wouldn't mean much if I wasn't as attracted to everything else about you, too. I've had the time to learn that I am. I love everything about you. I told you that I wasn't interested in what you have, but in what you have in here." She tapped her finger on the side of his head, and he smiled.

She placed her hand over his heart. "You've won me over with what's in here."

He took hold of her hand; a wave of heat rushed through her as he placed it over the front of his pants. "And now I want to thoroughly convince you with what's in here."

She ran her tongue over her bottom lip. She'd lain awake many a night over the last couple of weeks wondering what he'd be like as a lover. There were so many sides to him. She was eager to discover whether the vulnerable Seymour or the more persuasive one would show himself in the bedroom.

His eyes glimmered dark green when she looked into them. "Go ahead and convince me then," she said.

He held her hand as they walked up the stairs, and when he opened the bedroom door, she turned to look at him.

"What?"

"Don't worry. I didn't change my mind. It's just … you know how you said you like my house because it feels like me?"

He nodded.

"This room …" She stepped inside and looked around. It was a big room—there was a sitting area over by the windows, but it didn't look inviting. The bed and the furniture were all elaborately carved dark wood, but they looked like something out of a period drama to Chris. It wasn't a place you'd want to come and relax at the end of the day or to stay in bed on a Sunday morning. "It doesn't feel like you. I can see it being Seymour Davenport's room—you know, the humorless guy who they interview on the financial TV shows. But that's not the Seymour I know."

He stuck his bottom lip out and looked for all the world like a hurt child. "Humorless?"

She laughed. "You know what I mean. That Seymour is all business. I'm not trying to be mean, it's a beautiful room, but there's no warmth in it."

"I do know what you mean. And you're right, there's no warmth—or humor—in the man who's lived here. But I don't want to be that man anymore. I want to be the man I am when I'm with you."

He went and sat on the bed and held his hands out to her. She went to him and stood between his legs. He closed his arms around her and rested his head against her stomach. "This has only ever been the place where I come to sleep after work."

She tangled her fingers in his hair and held him against her, but he leaned back and looked up into her eyes. "Will you help me fill it with love and laughter? Make it a place where our grandkids want to come visit because it's a fun place to be?"

She nodded. She wasn't going to think too hard right now about whether her grandkids would ever visit this house. But she understood what he was asking, and she wanted to help him create it. "Let's start by filling it with love."

He reached up and pulled down the zipper on the back of her dress. She wriggled out of it and let it fall to her feet.

He looked like a starving man as he let his gaze move over her. "You're beautiful, Chris."

She unfastened the top button of his shirt and smiled when he helped by undoing the rest, then shrugging out of it. His chest was just like she'd imagined it would be. Broad and strong, muscled, dusted with gray.

He got to his feet and got rid of his pants before climbing onto the bed and reaching for her hand.

She lay down face to face with him and let out a little moan as he crushed her to his chest and buried his face in her neck. She let her hands wander over him, stroking his back and shoulders.

He lifted his head, and she cupped his face between her hands. "Kiss me."

When his lips came down on hers, she opened up to him, kissing him back, her tongue mating with his, her body quivering in anticipation. His hands moved over her, leaving trails of goose bumps in their wake. He unhooked her bra, and she got rid of it, turning to put it on the nightstand. When she turned back, the look in his eyes heated every cell in her body. The heat pooled between her legs as he closed his hands around her breasts.

He smiled at her as he caressed them. "I think you've caught me ogling these a time or two?"

She chuckled. "I haven't; I was starting to wonder if they didn't do it for you."

"Oh, they do it for me. Can I do it for them?"

"Do wha—"

He answered her by ducking his head and kissing each nipple in turn. They stood to attention, eager for more, and she lay back on the pillows surrendering to the sensations that his talented tongue sent racing through her.

She reached down and tugged at his boxers. She wanted them gone. He looked up but kept circling her nipples with his thumbs. "Are you in a hurry?" He cocked an eyebrow and gave her that quirky little smile.

"I want ..." She had to catch her breath as he tormented her nipples, squeezing just hard enough that it sent warning signals zipping through her, fanning the heat that was building between her legs.

"You want this?" He slid one hand inside her panties and stroked one finger over her entrance.

She nodded mutely.

He crawled back and slid down her panties, then stroked his hands back up over her thighs. She reached for him, hoping that he'd come back up and kiss her again and that their bodies could figure out between them how to fit together. He gave her a wicked smile and pushed her thighs farther apart. "May I?"

She stared at him. Did he plan to? He stroked his thumb over her, making her sigh. It'd been a long time since a man had taken any time or shown much interest in making sure she was ready. He dipped his head and trailed his tongue over her, making her grasp the sheets.

"You taste so sweet."

She rolled her eyes at the ceiling. Was he for real?

He was real, all right. And that talented tongue of his was working its magic. She rocked her hips in time with him as he tormented her, taking her closer and closer to the edge. She hadn't known if she'd be able to climax with him—it didn't always happen—but he was going to make sure she did. He seemed to understand what she needed better than she did herself. His fingers touching, his tongue dipping into her. Her muscles started to tense. She gripped the sheets harder.

"Seymour!" she gasped.

His response was to thrust his fingers deep, tipping her over the edge. She gasped her way through an orgasm stronger than she'd had in years. His fingers not letting her rest, his tongue urging her to give more, and she did.

When she finally lay still, he came up to lie beside her. He wrapped his arms around her and held her close.

She buried her face in his chest and closed her eyes.

"Are you okay?"

She nodded against him but didn't speak.

"Are you sure?" He sounded worried. "Was that not good?"

She forced herself to look up at him. "That was amazing! I'm embarrassed."

"Why?"

She shrugged. "I ... that was ... I didn't think. I didn't expect ..."

He smiled. She was starting to think of that as his cocky smile. His lips quirked up, and he looked pleased with himself. "You didn't expect to get there?"

She shook her head and then buried her face against his chest again. "Don't make me admit it! I'm not a spring chicken anymore."

He hugged her to him. "Nor would I want you to be. You're you, and you're beautiful. And you're so damned sexy."

"You really think so?"

He took hold of her hand and brought it down to touch him. She tried to bite back a smile, but she couldn't hide it. He was hot and hard—very hard.

"Does that tell you how much you turn me on?"

She nodded and closed her fingers around him, stroking up and down the length of him.

He closed his eyes and let his head fall back. She loved watching his face, loved knowing that she could give him so much pleasure. It wasn't enough, though. She wanted to give him the same kind of pleasure as he'd just given her. She started to move down the bed, but he caught her arm and rolled her onto her back.

"Don't you want ...?"

He chuckled. "I do, but maybe next time? This time is for both of us." He positioned himself above her and spread her legs with his knees.

She slid her arms up around his shoulders and closed her eyes as he used his hand to guide himself to her. The heat started to build again when his hot, hard head pushed into her.

He lowered his head and ran his tongue along her bottom lip. She opened up and kissed him back. His tongue thrust into her mouth and his body mirrored its movements. He thrust his hips, and she gasped as he filled her. She wrapped her legs around his, and her hips moved in time with his. He thrust deep and hard, carrying her away as he kissed her deeply. She grasped at his shoulders, doing what she could to hold on as he spun her away from reality and out into a space where only their bodies and pleasure existed. The pleasure mounted between her legs with every thrust; she could feel him grow harder and then tense. She moved with him desperately, not wanting to be left behind when his moment came. He lifted his head and slid his hands under her, kneading her backside, lifting her up to receive him, and when he did, he hit the spot and … "Seymour!" She gasped his name as he pushed her over the edge.

"Yes!" he cried as he followed her. She felt his release, carrying them both away. Wave after wave of pleasure crashed through her. She felt as though she dissolved and came back together around him in their frenzied coupling.

When they finally stilled, he smiled at her and planted a kiss on her lips. "You were well worth the wait, Chris."

She kissed the end of his nose. "So were you. But now that we know how good we are, we have some making up to do."

He chuckled and rolled to the side. "I like the sound of that. But you know I can't make it up to you if you're not in my bed."

She cocked her head to one side.

"I mean, it's going to be hard to make up for lost ground if I'm here and you're in Summer Lake."

Her heart sank. She couldn't come and be here with him. Her life was in Summer Lake—her kids, her grandkids.

He tucked his thumb under her chin and tilted her head back so she had to look him in the eye. "Don't look so worried. I don't want to be here anymore than I have to. What I'm saying is, I think it's time that I change things up—hand over the reins at work."

"Because of me?"

He touched her cheek. "Not so that I can follow you around every moment like a lost puppy dog if that's what you mean."

She let out a relieved laugh. "I wouldn't have put it that way."

"I do want to spend more time with you, Chris. But the changes I want to make are more inspired by you than for you. I doubt you'd want me under your feet the whole time."

She shook her head rapidly. For a moment there, she'd been afraid that he was going full-on needy guy.

"You put it into words for me. I need to save myself. I need to create new habits. I want you to be part of my life, Chris—a big part. But first, I need to figure out what my life should look like."

She smiled. "You do. I'll support you any way I can. I'll tease you and kick your butt when you need it. And hopefully, when you've figured it all out, you'll still have room for me. I want you to be a part of my life, too. I just won't be your next means of escape."

He curled his arm around her and held her close. "I don't need you to be my escape, Chris. I want you to be my new reality."

Chapter Fifteen

Seymour went to stand by the windows while he waited for the coffee to brew. He felt as though he was seeing the view with new eyes. Up until this weekend, he didn't remember ever taking the time to just stand here and take it in.

Usually, his Monday mornings here were short and hurried. He got up, showered, made coffee, and left for work. Today he'd followed the same routine, up to the leaving part. He wouldn't be doing that until Chris was ready, and she was still in the shower.

He smiled. The weekend had gone by so quickly. He wished it wasn't over yet. If she wasn't going to meet her sister, he would have asked her to stay. He wasn't sure if she would have agreed to it, but he would have asked.

He poured two mugs of coffee and sipped his own. He drank it as it came—black, no sugar. He didn't know what he should add to Chris's. In small, practical respects like that, there was still so much he had to learn about her. But he knew everything he needed to know about the way she made him feel. And about the changes he wanted to make in his life.

She came bounding down the stairs looking like summer in a pair of white slacks and a bright blue blouse.

"I hope that's coffee?"

"Yes. Decaf, that's all I drink."

She stopped dead halfway across the kitchen, and the smile froze on her face. "Decaf?"

He had to laugh. "No. I'm pulling your leg."

"Phew!" She came to him and took the mug he held out to her. "I should warn you, I don't take many things seriously, but my morning coffee is one of them."

"Duly noted. Do you want cream and sugar?"

"No, thanks. I'm sweet enough."

He went to her and pecked her lips. "You are."

She put the mug down and slid her arms around his waist. "I had such a great time this weekend."

He held her close to his chest. "I did, too. Is it still okay if I come to see you next weekend?"

"Yes. I can't wait!"

"Neither can I. I'm going to be busy this week, but if I can get finished up in time, would you mind if I come before the weekend?"

"Not at all. I wish you could come with me now."

He chuckled. "You're not even going home yourself yet."

"You know what I mean, though." She looked up into his eyes, and his heart buzzed with happiness. "I wish we didn't have to say goodbye again today."

"I hope the day will come when we don't ever say goodbye again."

She nodded. "I do, too."

"I love you, Chris."

"And I love you; don't doubt that. I do hope we can figure this out. But I'm a practical soul. We both have lives and commitments that we're not going to give up. And much as I love spending time with you, I need time for myself, too."

His heart sank. This weekend had been so much fun; they'd been so happy together. Was she trying to let him down gently now that it was over? Or was she simply telling him not to get too carried away?

"Don't look like that. I just told you, I love you. I want to be with you. But for both our sakes, whatever we're going to build together, we need to build carefully. We need to make sure that there's room for each of us still to be ourselves."

"Okay. For a minute there, I thought you were telling me …" He hesitated, not sure what he'd thought.

She planted a peck on his lips. "I'm telling myself as much as I'm telling you that, great as this all is, we don't want to spoil it by rushing it."

She looked over his shoulder, making him smile because he knew what she was doing. "How are we for time?"

She chuckled. "I've got plenty. It's you I'm thinking about. I bet you're normally at the office by now, aren't you?"

"I am. But recently, I met this beautiful woman who taught me to play things by ear. I'll get there when I get there today." And after this week, he wasn't sure how much he'd go there at all. It was time to restructure. He wouldn't step down completely, but it was time to put someone else at the helm and take more of a back seat.

She sipped her coffee. "Okay, but I don't want to make you miss too much of your day. And the sooner we go, the more time I'll have to hang out with Ivan before Marianne arrives."

He laughed. "What do you and Ivan plan to do?"

She grinned. "I'm going to ask him to walk on the pier with me. It's not far from the airport, and I've heard a lot about it from the kids, but I've never been there." She raised an eyebrow at him. "I'll bet you haven't either, have you?"

"Not for ..." He stopped at the sound of his cell phone ringing. He didn't want to take the call, didn't want to let work intrude on the last of his time with her.

She made a face at him. "I'd guess you need to take that, and I need to get my things together. I'll meet you back here in a few." He watched her take her coffee and go back upstairs before he answered the call. He was surprised how much he'd rather switch the phone off, forget work, and go for that walk on the pier with her.

Chris looked out of the window as the plane climbed away from the Santa Monica airport. She smiled at the sight of the pier. That had been a fun walk. She hoped she'd be able to go back there with Seymour one day soon. He needed that kind of fun in his life. She caught one of her bags before it slid under her feet.

Marianne smiled at her. "You're looking very pleased with yourself."

Chris looked down at the bag. "I am. I didn't plan to buy much, but I couldn't resist. I love Holly's store at the plaza, but the original Hayes store has so much more. And Roberto is such a sweetheart. He knew just what suited me and found things I'd never have chosen for myself."

"He's amazing, isn't he? I'm glad we stopped in there."

"We needed it after all those snooty bridal places."

Marianne made a face. "Yeah, that wasn't as much fun as I hoped it would be. I guess they prefer their brides younger and slimmer."

Chris waved a hand at her. "Screw them, then. It worked out for the best."

"Thanks to Roberto again."

"Yep, and now you have the biggest item marked off your list. Is everything else coming together for the wedding?"

"It is. I can't wait, Chris. And I'd put money on you and Seymour not being far behind us."

Chris nodded slowly.

"What? You don't agree?"

She shrugged. "I can see it. I'm just not sure if I want it."

Marianne leaned forward in her seat. "Why? I thought everything was going wonderfully. From what you've said about the weekend. From the way you look when you talk about him … I thought it was inevitable."

"And it could be. I don't know. Don't get me wrong. He's wonderful. And I love him. I'm not even afraid to admit it. But there's a long road between here and there."

"And what landmarks do you need to pass on that road?"

"Just one big one. He says that he's ready to step back from his job. He won't give it up completely; I wouldn't want him to—he wouldn't know what to do with himself. But you have to remember, I've been in this position before."

Marianne looked puzzled.

"I've been in love with a man who wanted to give up his addiction and build a better life with me. Remember how that worked out?"

"Of course, I do. But this is different. Seymour's a workaholic, not an alcoholic. He's hardly likely to … he's not that kind of man. And besides, working all the time wouldn't make him violent or angry."

"I'm not saying it would. I'm not even talking about the worst aspects of it. What I'm saying is that I don't want to wait around believing that he wants to build a life with me when he can't do it. When there's always something else that he'd rather be doing. I don't need all his time or attention—I wouldn't want it—but I do want to know that we're in it together. I won't wait on the sidelines while he hides from his demons in his work. I don't want to be with him unless he's wrestled all his demons and beaten them. I'm in a good place; I've done the work. I need to be sure that he's done his."

Marianne shook her head. "And you think that because he's so eager to go all-in with you that he hasn't? That he should take more time first?"

"I guess. I don't even want him to take more time. I'd love for us to just be able to move forward and figure out what sharing life might look like for us. I'm cautious, that's all."

"Well, there's nothing wrong with a bit of caution. But don't let it hold you back from jumping into a new life. You've set yourself up well since you came to the lake. But don't cling to it so hard that you refuse to grab onto something better."

"I suppose." Chris stared out the window again. Was that what she was doing? Clinging tightly to the life she'd built for herself, afraid to open it up and let Seymour in? She didn't think so. She wanted him to come into her life—but she didn't want to turn it upside down for him.

~ ~ ~

Seymour sat back and looked around the room. A lot of surprised faces stared back at him.

"Questions?"

Darren Porter, one of the senior analysts, held his gaze for a long moment, then asked, "So, the only major change will be Alan taking over your day-to-day responsibilities?"

Seymour nodded. "In terms of how it will affect all of you, yes." He smiled at Alan. "I imagine it will mean a slight change of direction for the fund since Alan thinks differently than I do."

There were a few murmurs around the table, but he held up a hand. "It's no secret that the risk managers will be pleased with the change."

Alan laughed beside him. "I admit that I'm not as aggressive as you." He smiled around the room. "Seymour may be the one taking an early retirement of sorts, but I think the rest of us will live a bit longer—less chance of heart attacks—once we change tack."

He was greeted with a few chuckles, but some eyes turned in Seymour's direction. He knew that the company was fairly evenly split between aggressive risk-takers like himself and more conservative types like Alan. Overall, it made for a good balance, and the portfolio reflected that. He knew that stepping down wouldn't create a major shift in direction, but it would pull them back from some of the more volatile markets. It was a good thing, and he knew it. He'd walked a very fine line for a long time. He could see now that he'd been selfish. He'd kept the company on a knife edge because doing so required all of his attention—and left very little of him or his time to invest in the rest of his life.

Alan was right—stress and blood pressure levels would no doubt drop significantly around here once Alan was at the helm. Seymour had every faith in him. They'd worked together for over fifteen years now. He deserved this opportunity, and Seymour was happy to give it to him.

It seemed strange to walk out of the office at two in the afternoon, but he smiled when he saw Ivan waiting at the curb for him.

Ivan grinned back at him. "Is this it, then? Did you do it?"

He grinned back. "I did. I don't know what happens next, but you don't need to bring me in here tomorrow. Or any day. We'll still come in sometimes. I'm not stepping down completely, but the days of you dropping me off here every morning and picking me up again late at night to take me home again are over."

"That's awesome." Ivan held the door open for him, but Seymour grinned, and instead, slid into the passenger seat.

Ivan came around and smiled at him as he buckled himself in. "So, that's how it is, now then, huh?"

"It is. Where do you want to go?"

Ivan laughed. "I thought you'd want to go home?"

"Not yet. Although, I don't know … yes, I do. I know it'll be the second time for you this week, but do you want to go to Santa Monica, to the pier?"

Ivan laughed. "Sure. Miss Chris was saying on Monday that she wished you could go out there."

"Well, I should make her wish come true."

Ivan's mood seemed somber as they neared Santa Monica.

"Anything you want to tell me?"

Ivan glanced over at him. "I'm wondering if there's anything *you* want to tell me?"

"Not that I can think of. Why?"

"Don't feel bad if you need to let me go now. I understand. It doesn't make sense to keep me on."

"No!" Seymour was startled by the suggestion. "No way. I don't want to lose you. Just because I won't be going to the office every day anymore … That doesn't mean … Relax. I have no intention of letting you go. It hadn't even crossed my mind."

Ivan gave him a half smile. "Thanks. But it's not just about driving you to the office, is it? I drive you because you're always so damned busy with your investments or whatever it is you do. You're getting out of that game to free up your time— to be present in your own life. Most people drive themselves around in their own lives."

"I know. I understand that. But …" He shook his head. "We'll figure something out. I'll admit I did enjoy driving when we were at the lake. But there's no way I'm letting you go. We're restructuring, that's all." He frowned. Ivan was right. If he was going to live the kind of life he wanted to, he wouldn't need a driver. But he wasn't going to repay Ivan's support and encouragement by firing him. "It's not as though you only drive. You take care of the houses; you take care of all kinds of practical details."

Ivan gave him a rueful smile. "Details that most people take care of themselves."

"I never claimed to be normal. I'm not freeing up my time so I can mire myself in those kinds of details. I'm going to do more with the charities; I'm going to see where I can contribute in this life and work on that. I'm not going to sit home on my ass all day."

Ivan chuckled. "I didn't think you were. I just wanted to let you know, I'll understand if you need to let me go."

"Well, I don't. Subject closed. Unless you want out?"

Ivan shook his head. "I don't, but I don't want to be kept around as a charity case either."

"You know me better than that."

"I do."

"We'll figure it out. I'm still going to be spending time here, at the house, and at the office. I'll still be in Montana around the family a good bit, and I'm hoping that Summer Lake will become the place I call home."

"I'd like that, too."

Seymour cocked an eyebrow at him. "You like it there?"

"I do."

"You like someone there?"

"Maybe."

Seymour chuckled. "In that case, maybe I should set up an office there. Bring in a small staff to oversee the charity work. You could head it up, if you'd enjoy that?"

"Just like that?" Ivan looked skeptical.

"Why not?"

Ivan pulled into a parking lot a couple of blocks from the pier. "Do you want to walk from here?"

"Sure. And while we walk, we talk about what our new office in Summer Lake should look like."

Chapter Sixteen

"Are you sure you don't mind?" asked Emma.

"Of course, I don't." Chris took hold of Isabel's hand. "We're going to have fun, aren't we, sweet pea?"

Isabel smiled up at her. "We're going to the park."

"That's right." Chris looked back at Emma. "You'd better get going."

Emma checked her watch. "I had. And Jack said he'll come and collect her from you as soon as he gets finished at work."

"There's no rush. You know I love spending time with her. Relax. It's not a problem. It's not Jack's fault he got caught up at the office."

Emma smiled. "I know. I'm sorry. I shouldn't get stressed about it. But you're always so organized; I hate asking you at the last minute like this."

"You can ask me any time you like. I'll drop anything to help you out."

"I know—and that's what bothers me. You wouldn't tell me if you had other plans, you'd just drop them. But don't worry, I won't ask you anything this weekend. Seymour's coming, isn't he?"

"He is."

Emma clasped her hands together. "I'm keeping my fingers and toes crossed for you."

Chris laughed. "Thank you. But you'd better uncross them and get going, or you're going to be late. I can lock up on our way out."

"Oh! You're right." Emma glanced at the clock on the wall. "I'd better go."

Chris picked Isabel up, and they waved as they watched Emma back out of the driveway.

"Come on, sweet pea. Let's get your things into Grandma's car."

Once she had Isabel's car seat set up and a few of her favorite things in with her, Chris locked up the house. Emma had called her in a panic just as she was leaving the women's center. Jack was supposed to be finishing work early to watch Isabel, but he was caught up in a meeting. Chris had driven up here to their place so that Emma could still leave on time for a meeting of her own.

Once they were on the road, Chris glanced at Isabel in the rearview mirror. She was holding her favorite bear close to her chest and kissing the top of his head, murmuring something to him.

"Are you and Teddy okay?"

Isabel smiled at her. "Teddy's happy."

"Why's that?"

"He likes Grandma's house, and he likes the park."

Chris chuckled. Teddy had a lot of likes and dislikes. He tended to be the spokesperson for wants too. *Teddy wants ice cream* was a familiar plea at her house.

She decided to go straight to the park. It would still be quiet before the kids got out of school. She preferred to have the place to themselves than to have to explain to Isabel what the bigger kids were doing.

They were walking down the path by the duck pond when her phone rang. She made a face, wondering if she should ignore it. Much as she disliked intrusions on her time with Isabel, she pulled it out of her purse. Her heart beat a little faster when she saw Seymour's name on the display.

"Hello. This is a pleasant surprise. What's up?"

"Nothing's up. I just wanted to hear your voice." He sounded hesitant, uncertain maybe.

"It's good to hear you, too. What are you up to?"

"That's what I wanted to ask you. What are you doing right now?"

"I'm at the park with Isabel."

"Oh."

"Why?" He sounded disappointed, and she didn't understand why he would be.

"No reason. I … What are you doing this evening?"

"Jack's coming to pick her up after work, and then I'll probably get some dinner at the Boathouse. This young lady will probably wear me out, so I won't feel like cooking. What are you … wait, you're not here, are you?" It was Thursday. He'd said he might come back before the weekend if he could.

He chuckled. "I just landed. I was going to tell you that I was thinking of coming today when we talked last night, but I wasn't sure if it would work out. Don't worry, though. I won't intrude on your time with Isabel. If you like, you can call me later—let me know what time you're going to the Boathouse for dinner, and I'll meet you there."

She laughed. "We did this once already. I don't want to mess it up again, so let's be upfront about it, shall we? I would love for you to come and hang out with Isabel and me if you'd like to."

"You would?"

"Yes. Do you want to?"

"I'd love to."

"Why don't you come and join us at the park then. Do you know where it is?"

"I have no idea."

"Well, when you get on Main Street, you come past the resort and keep on going. The street changes, it gets broader and quieter, and the houses are bigger, but it's still Main. You go all the way to the end, and there's a little parking area. You'll see my car there. Then you follow the path, and it'll bring you past the duck pond and then on to the swings. Depending on how long you take we'll be in one of those places."

"Great. I won't be long."

"Okay. We'll see you in a little while." Chris hung up and put her phone back in her purse.

Isabel tugged her hand. "Who's that?"

"That was Grandma's friend, Seymour. He's going to come and play with us."

Isabel scowled. "Okay." She didn't look too happy about it, but she tugged on Chris's hand. "Swings."

Chris pushed her on the swings for a little while until she got bored and wanted to go back to see the ducks. Chris was glad that she'd grabbed the baggie of bread crusts on her way out of her house earlier. She always kept a bag in the fridge for occasions like today when Jack and Emma needed her to step in and help out.

Chris sat on the bench and chuckled to herself as Isabel threw bread at the ducks.

She glanced over at the parking area, wondering how long it would be before Seymour showed up and whether it had been a good idea to invite him to join them. She didn't see why it wouldn't be.

Isabel came and put her hands on her knees. "Grandma's house."

"Okay." Chris got to her feet. Isabel was one of those kids who went and went and went like a windup toy, but when she wound down, she got cranky and sleepy very quickly. "Let's go back to the car."

Seymour appeared through the gap in the hedge just before they reached it. He stopped and smiled when he saw them, then hurried forward.

"Hey. I'm sorry it took me a while. I wanted to get Ivan set up with a cabin."

"You brought Ivan?"

"Yes, but I'll explain later." He smiled down at Isabel. "Hello."

She looked at him then at Chris, then wrapped her arms around Chris's knees.

"It's okay, Isabel. This is my friend. This is Seymour."

Isabel looked up at her. "Grandma's house."

"We're going. But say hello to Seymour first." Chris picked her up so that she was on eye level with him.

"Hello, Isabel."

She looked him over very carefully and then rested her head against Chris's cheek. "Hello."

Chris heaved a sigh of relief. She'd had a feeling that Isabel was too tired and too cranky to meet a stranger. Luckily, she was too tired to play up, too.

She smiled at Seymour. "We're about done here. This little madam needs a nap. Do you want to follow me back to my place?"

"Sure." He waited while she got Isabel strapped into her seat. When she straightened up, he pecked her cheek. "I'm sorry it took me so long."

She slipped her arms around his waist. "Don't be. That's something you'll have to get used to around here. Plans are flexible, mini emergencies crop up—like me having her this afternoon. It's all good."

"Thanks. It is good now that I'm here. I missed you, Chris."

"I missed you, too. I want to hear all about your week. How things went at the office—and why Ivan's here."

"I'll tell you all about it. But do you think we should get Isabel home first?" He waggled his fingers at her, and she gave him a sleepy smile. "She looks like she's about to conk out right there."

"You're right. Let's get her home first."

Seymour loved watching Chris with little Isabel. She was so sweet and patient with her, yet firm. She set her down for a nap when they got back to the house, and just as Chris came into the kitchen where he was waiting for her, Isabel started to cry.

Chris shrugged. "She's absolutely fine."

"Don't you want to go and check?"

"Want to? Of course, I do. I want to go and get her out of bed and hold her and rock her and tell her Grandma's there for her until she falls asleep." She chuckled. "It's not about what I want, though, unfortunately. It's about what's best for her."

Cries continued to set Seymour's nerves on edge for another few moments, and then they subsided and stopped.

"See? Now she'll get a good nap. If I'd gone in there, she'd have stayed awake and made herself even more tired and then she'd have fallen asleep later and woken up later and then be a grouchy little madam for her daddy later."

Seymour smiled. "You're right. You're good at this, aren't you?"

"I learned with the boys. It's harder to be as strict with myself now that I don't have to deal with the consequences. But it's all about what's best for her. That's all I care about."

He went to her and closed his arms around her waist, dropping a kiss on her forehead. "You're a good woman, Chris."

"Thank you. And you're a good man. I've missed you."

"I missed you more." Having her in his arms again woke his body up to just how much he'd missed her—and how pleased he was to see her again.

She must have sensed it. She pressed her hips against his and looked up into his eyes with a little laugh. "You're also a hard man—and a hard man is good to find."

He laughed and held her closer. "I'm looking forward to reminding you how good I am later."

"Modest, aren't you?"

"Just honest. You told me loud enough and often enough last weekend just how good you thought I was."

She pushed at his arm but didn't look embarrassed. He was glad about that. The first time he made her come for him, she'd hidden her face from him. Over the course of the weekend, she'd gotten over it. She'd screamed her appreciation that last time on Sunday night, and he was hoping she'd do the same tonight.

She looked around. "Where's your bag? You are still going to stay with me, aren't you?"

"I am. I want to. I didn't want to assume, though. And I didn't know how Jack would feel about it, so I left my bag in the car, just in case."

She laughed. "I didn't think about that. You're going to be here when Jack comes to pick Isabel up. He wouldn't dare say anything. He knows you're coming this weekend."

"And he knows I'm staying with you?"

She dropped her gaze. "It's not that I didn't want to tell him."

"That's okay. I know it's better to choose your moment."

She made a face at him. "It shouldn't be though. He should be happy for me."

"And I'm sure he will be, once he gets used to the idea, and once he gets to know me better and can trust that I'm going to be good to you."

"I know, thank you. I shouldn't get mad at him for it. Anyway. Do you want a drink? I have soda or …"

"Water's good for me. Can I get it? Can I get you anything?" She cocked her head to one side, and he laughed. "If I'm going to be staying here with you, then I don't want you treating me as a guest. This is about us being together, isn't it?"

She nodded. "I guess."

"If we were going to move into a place together, we'd both pull our weight. Just because I'm coming into your place, I don't expect you to wait on me."

She held his gaze for a long moment, and he wondered if she was going to argue. She didn't. Instead, she pulled out a stool at the counter and sat down. "In that case, I'll take a lemonade."

~ ~ ~

Despite what she'd said earlier, Chris was a little nervous when she heard Jack's car pull up outside. She cast a glance at Seymour, who was sitting on the floor, surrounded by Isabel's soft toys. She was standing in front of him, tapping on her little whiteboard easel.

He grinned at her. "I think she's the teacher and we," he looked around at the stuffed animals, "are the class."

Isabel gave him a stern look and tapped on the whiteboard again.

Chris laughed. "Well, I'll leave you to it then. Don't get yourself a detention. I'm going to let Jack in."

She hurried to the front door and went out to meet him halfway up the path.

"Hey, Mom. Thanks for this. I'm sorry." He bent down to kiss her cheek.

"There's no need to apologize, you know I love having her, and I love helping you guys out. She's made a new friend this afternoon, too. Seymour. He's here."

Jack frowned. "He's here already? I knew he was coming this weekend, but ... I'm sorry. Did I mess up your plans with him?"

"Not at all. I didn't know he was coming today. It was a surprise."

Jack smiled through pursed lips. "But the surprise turned out to be on him. Instead of getting you a day early, he got an Isabel more than he bargained for."

She laughed. "Yeah, but he's been a good sport. She likes him."

"She does? She's a good judge of character."

"Come on in and see for yourself. I just wanted to warn you—and to ask you to go easy. He's important to me, Jack."

"How important?"

"Very."

He raised an eyebrow. "Very as in, I need to get to know him?"

She nodded. "You do. He's going to be spending a lot of time here."

"At the lake?"

She looked back at the house then at Jack again. "Here."

He wrapped his arms around her for a brief moment. "Okay, then. If this is what you want. I'm behind you every step of the way. I'll treat him as your man—until he proves he doesn't deserve to be."

"Come on."

When they went back into the living room, Chris's heart melted when she saw Isabel sitting on Seymour's knee. Her little arm was slung around his neck as they both looked down at the book he was holding.

She glanced at Jack and knew that Seymour had just taken his first steps into Jack's good books.

Seymour smiled up at them. "I think I'm in class." He nodded at the whiteboard. "All the teddy bears were able to follow along, but I think I'm getting remedial lessons."

Jack laughed. "I feel you. The bears always get it before I do, too."

Isabel waved the book in front of Seymour's face, drawing his attention back to her.

"Look who's here, Isabel," said Chris.

"Hello, Daddy."

Chris had to laugh. Usually, she came flying to Jack when he arrived, but it seemed she was more interested in teaching her new student.

"Isabel?"

She looked at Jack.

"Do I get a kiss?"

She smiled at him but didn't move.

"What are you doing?"

"Seesaw!"

Jack gave Chris a puzzled look. "Seesaw?"

She laughed. "I think she means Seymour."

She nodded happily and patted Seymour's cheek. "Seesaw."

Jack laughed. "Welcome to the family, Seesaw."

His words shocked Chris, and she could tell they shocked Seymour, too. She watched the two men exchange a look that she didn't quite understand. All she knew was that she wasn't going to have to worry about Jack giving him a hard time anymore.

Chapter Seventeen

Seymour tightened his arm around Chris's shoulders, and she turned to smile up at him.

"Are you okay?" she asked.

"That's what I'm trying to tell you. Sitting here, holding you. I'm better than I've been in a long time—maybe ever."

She snuggled into his side. "Maybe small-town life suits you."

"Maybe it does. Maybe you suit me."

That was how it felt to him. She suited him. The way she was—with him, with everyone around her, mostly with herself. She was just so straightforward, so competent. She put him at ease in a way he hadn't known was possible.

Hanging out with her and Isabel this afternoon—and later with Jack for a little while—it had been wonderful, so comfortable. They weren't doing anything that was going to change the world, or even change anyone's fortunes. But they were doing something significant—something he'd forgotten how to do—if he'd ever known. They were just living life. Teaching a new little person how to live her life. It was all stuff he wouldn't have given a second thought to a few years ago. Now it was everything that mattered.

"I'd like to think so." She smiled up at him. "Do I suit you enough to make you think that you could maybe stick around here?"

"So much that I don't think I ever want to leave."

She sat up and gave him a puzzled look. Her smile gone.

"Relax. That's how I feel in this moment. I'd soon grow restless if I never left—and besides, Hope's in Montana, so are Dylan and Chance. I still have other places I need to be. But this is the first time I've felt that I could just relax into living life and not have to keep moving."

"Sorry. I didn't mean that I want you to leave." She touched his cheek. "Or even that I wouldn't want you to stay forever. It just worries me. I don't want you to see this place—especially not me—as a little escape bubble. You know?"

"I do. I get it. But I promise you, that's not what I'm doing. I'm not getting all caught up in the buzz of it and not wanting to go back to reality—not like I did with work, not like what happens with booze."

She stared at him. Maybe he shouldn't have made reference to her husband, but he was trying to make the point that this was different.

"I don't want to stay here to escape my reality. I want to create a new reality—with you."

"Can you really see yourself staying here with me?"

"Yes. And I'm not even sure what you mean. But yes, to all the possibilities. I can see myself staying here—in this small town, that not so long ago I would have told you I wouldn't last more than a week in. I can see myself staying here in your house. I love this place, Chris. It feels like you. I like the way you live here. I want to live this way. It's straightforward. It doesn't need *stuff.*"

She gave him a questioning look, and he chuckled. "You commented on all the *stuff* at my house. The driveway, the view, the pool, the chandelier."

She smiled. "Ah, yes. That *stuff.* The stuff that costs a lot of money but doesn't hold any value."

He nodded. "Exactly. There's so much more value here. In your house, with little Isabel and Jack earlier."

"I could have spent this afternoon in the office and closed a position that made several million dollars. And I know now that I got more value for my time by spending it here with you and your family."

She touched his cheek. "You really mean that, don't you?"

"I do. I finally get it. It's taken me more than half a century, but I get it now. And since I don't know how many more years I have left, I intend to put every day to good use." He dropped a kiss on her lips. "I want to spend as many of my days as I can with you."

She slid her arms up around his neck and pulled him down into a kiss.

As always, her kisses sent desire coursing through his veins. She was bringing him back to life in so many ways. She made him want to be present in his life and to live it for what truly mattered. She also made him want to reaffirm life in the most basic way he knew how.

Her fingers tangled in his hair as she kissed him, making his scalp tingle and sending ripples down his spine. He didn't want to wait until later, and he didn't want to break the intensity of the moment by asking if she wanted to go to bed.

He let his hands move over her, touching her plump breasts through her top, grasping her ass and holding her against him as he rocked his hips.

She told him what he needed to know when she untucked his shirt and pushed it up so she could run her hands over his chest. He bit down on his bottom lip when she tweaked his nipples between her fingers and thumbs. He hadn't known they were so sensitive! It spurred him on, his sense of urgency growing as he pushed her skirt up around her waist.

She pulled her top off and unhooked the front fastener of her bra. He couldn't resist cupping her breasts in his hands and dipping his head to tease her nipples to attention with his tongue. They soon stood proud and erect. Much like his cock was trying to do inside his pants.

Chris seemed to hear his thoughts and unzipped his jeans, pushing them down over his hips. She slid her hand inside his boxers, closing her fingers around him and making him groan as she began to work her hand up and down the length of him.

He slid one hand between her legs, hooking a finger inside her panties and pulling them aside so he could touch her. He wanted to give her all the time she needed, but if she kept working him the way she was, it might not work out.

He moved his hips away, and she relinquished her hold on him.

"You don't like it?"

"I like it a little too much and I want to make sure we're on the same page."

She averted her gaze.

"We can take our time." As he traced her entrance with his fingers, he knew she needed a little more time.

She blew out a sigh. "You're sweet. But I don't want to need more time. I want to be able to jump on you, right now."

He couldn't help but smile at the determination with which she said it. "You're going to jump on me?"

She gave him a rueful smile. "Eventually, maybe." She rubbed herself against his fingers. "If you quit talking about it and keep that up."

"If I have to quit talking, you'd better lie back and close your eyes."

"Ooh! I like the sound of that." She did as he said.

He reached for his half-empty glass of water that stood on the coffee table and dipped his fingers inside it. "Are you keeping your eyes shut?"

"Yes! But I'm going to have to peek soon. What are you doing?"

He stroked his wet fingers over her and circled her clit.

"Oh! What? Oh!" She opened her eyes, and he smiled, loving the way her cheeks and chest flushed with pleasure.

"Close your eyes."

She lay back and did as she was told.

He grew hard as a rock as he kept dipping his fingers in the water and touching her. He circled her nipples, causing them to pebble and tighten. He trailed droplets up her inner thighs and traced her lips. She writhed and moaned until he finally dipped a finger inside her, and she gasped. "Yes! Seymour. Now!"

He didn't want to waste any time getting rid of the rest of their clothes. He held her panties to the side and positioned himself between her legs. He pushed slowly at first, almost losing it as she welcomed him inside. She was hot and slick for him. He grasped her hips and thrust deep.

"Oh, God, yes!"

Her cries urged him on as they moved together. She clenched tight around him, giving him the sensation that he might lose himself inside her and never come back.

Her legs came up to wrap around his and her hands scrabbled at his back. He picked up the pace, holding her hips as she took him deeper and deeper.

It started at the bottom of his spine, the pressure of so much pent-up desire ignited and drove him on, keeping up a frantic rhythm that could reach only one conclusion. He felt her tighten around him; she was close. He buried his face in her neck and grazed the soft skin there with his teeth.

It had the effect he desired. Her nails raked down his shoulder as she let herself go. "Seymour!"

Her inner muscles drew him in deeper and deeper until all the pressure inside him found its release. He saw stars as he let himself go with her, carrying each other away on waves of sheer pleasure.

When he finally slumped down on her chest, she tangled her fingers in his hair and smiled at him.

"I think I need to tell you to quit talking more often."

He chuckled. "I'm not sure I'll ever speak again."

"Do you want to go out for breakfast?" asked Seymour.

Chris thought about it. She did sometimes take a walk over to the resort on a Sunday morning to see who was around. Emma and Jack went sometimes; Missy and Dan were usually there. There was a crowd of their friends who go together whenever they could, and she liked to hang out with them sometimes. She didn't feel like it today, though.

It had turned out to be quite a sociable weekend. They'd gone to the Boathouse on Friday night, had lunch with Marianne and Clay yesterday, and been invited over to Dan and Missy's place last night. That had been fun. Most of the boys' friends had been there. She'd been surprised to see Ivan and Adam there as well, but she probably shouldn't have been. Newcomers were always welcomed into the fold.

Seymour came and hugged her to him. "Sorry, I didn't realize it was a question that would need so much thought."

She laughed. "It doesn't. I don't want to go. I'm a social creature, but I've had enough social time this weekend. I'd rather have you to myself."

"Want me to make us something?"

"No. I think we should get in the car, stop by the bakery for sandwiches on our way out of town, and go for a hike."

"That sounds perfect."

Half an hour later they were heading up East Shore Road. Seymour looked out of the window at the lake. "This is how life should be."

She laughed. "This is how life is."

"You're right. This is my life now. My mind's not half-focused on what I'm going to do tomorrow. What needs to happen at work. I'm just right here with you." He reached across and squeezed her leg as she drove. "And there's nowhere else I'd rather be."

A few minutes later, she turned off and followed a dirt road up into the foothills. She brought the car to a stop at the trailhead.

"Do you hike up here a lot?"

"Sometimes. Usually on a Sunday. It's peaceful and so beautiful. You wait until you see the views from farther up."

As they made their way up the path through the pines, Seymour took hold of her hand. "And you usually come up here all by yourself?"

"Yep. Marianne came along a couple of times, but she has other things to do with her time these days."

"Have things changed between the two of you now that she's with Clay?"

Chris thought about it. "Not much, no. She's happier than I've ever known her. I love that for her. Clay's a good guy, and he's good for her. Obviously, she spends most of her time with him, but she still does her own thing. We still have lunch at least once a week, and we still go for nights out at the Boathouse. Sometimes, he comes along, too. He's not here all the time, though. He goes back to Nashville at least once a month."

"And she doesn't go with him?"

"Sometimes. He goes to work, and she has her own life to be getting on with here."

"So, that part of his life is still separate?"

Chris went ahead as the path narrowed and held a branch to let him go by before she spoke again. "Not really. She goes with him sometimes, but she's made her own friends there. She goes to see Shawnee, and she spends time with Autumn, too. Do you know them?"

"Not well. I know Shawnee Reynolds, more through her music than personally. I've met Autumn and her sister Summer. Summer lives in Paradise Valley—where Hope and Chance live."

"Oh, of course. It really is a small world, isn't it?"

"It is. When you stop and think about all the people we have in common, it's amazing."

She nodded. "What's with all the questions anyway?"

He walked beside her again as the path emerged from the trees, and a broad meadow opened before them. "I'm not being nosey about Marianne and Clay. I'm curious about how they make it work." He took hold of her hand. "I'm thinking about how we're going to make this work."

She smiled up at him. "We'll figure it out as we go along."

He chuckled. "I had a feeling you might say that."

Chris pointed to a fallen log at the edge of the meadow. "Do you want to sit over there and eat our breakfast?"

She sat on the log, and he sat on the ground, looking up at her. She handed him a sandwich and a bottle of water. "How do you want this to work?" she asked.

"I want to be with you, Chris. That's as much as I know for certain. I know your life is here. I'd like for my life to be based here, but …" he blew out a sigh. "I can't just walk out on the rest of my life. I don't want to."

"I don't see why you would."

"I suppose I'm thinking that way because of my tendency to go all-in on anything I do."

She smiled. "You can be with me and not have to spend every waking—and sleeping—moment with me. I don't think I'd last very long if you wanted to."

"I understand that. But I'll still have to go back to Malibu sometimes. I want to keep spending time in Montana with Hope and Chance and Dylan. I have a house in the Caymans."

She raised an eyebrow at him. "What do you do there? I already know you're not big on hanging out at the beach."

He gave her a rueful smile. "I have meetings there sometimes. It's about being where my people are again. I golf when I'm there."

She made a face at him. "Because you enjoy it?"

He laughed. "Because it's an accepted means of doing business. You'd be surprised how many deals are made on the golf course."

She shook her head. "Well, there's no reason you can't keep doing all of those things. I'll still be here when you get back."

"You wouldn't want to go with me?"

"Maybe. Sometimes. But not every time. I don't need to follow you around while you live your life—just like you don't have to wait around here while I live mine."

He nodded. "And you think that can work? Like it does for Marianne and Clay?"

"I do. We're not kids struck with young love that makes us want to spend all our time together."

"No."

"I think we can share enough that we feel connected and do enough by ourselves that we'll have plenty to tell each other about."

"I like the sound of that. I hope you won't mind if I'm here more than you expect, though?"

She reached out and touched his cheek. "I'll love every moment that you're here. But don't try to force it. You don't have anything to do here. You'd go nuts just hanging around."

"I am going to have lots to do here, though. I'm going to set up an office."

She choked on her sandwich and had to take a gulp of soda to wash it down.

"Are you okay?"

She cleared her throat. "I am. What kind of office?"

He chuckled. "I thought that would surprise you, but I didn't expect you to choke on it. I've decided I need a headquarters

for my charity work. I used to do it alongside my work in
Malibu. I had an office, I had all the admin support I needed,
and I carved out the time. Now I have all the time I need, but
not the office or staff.

"Ivan's going to head it up for me. I'm not going to need
him to drive me around much anymore, but I don't want to let
him go. What do you think?"

She leaned down and dropped a kiss on his lips. "I think
that's a wonderful idea."

"I hoped you might."

"You should talk to Renee. I don't know much about how
she set up the women's center, but she'd be able to give you
some ideas."

"Thanks. I'll see if she can spare any time for me this week.
Ivan and I are going to be working with a realtor this week to
find a suitable space we can lease."

"Which realtor?"

"Austin … something or other. Clay recommended him."

Chris laughed. "He's a good guy."

"Let me guess, he's another friend of Jack and Dan's?"

"That's right."

"Well, at least I know I'm in good hands."

"You are. How long do you plan to stay?"

He met her gaze. "How long do you want me?"

"As long as you want to be here."

He took hold of her hand and squeezed it. "Is there
something you're not telling me?"

"No. Yes." She made a face at him. "I'm thrilled you're here.
I'm thrilled you want to stay. My concern is that the novelty of
staying in my little house with me will wear off soon."

"It won't, Chris. I feel more at home in your house with you than I do in any of my houses."

"You won't miss all your stuff?"

He chuckled. "Not a bit. As you pointed out, I didn't use most of it anyway. I didn't have it because it meant something to me, only because it was expensive, and I lived an expensive life. Here, with you, it's not about having expensive things. It's about having valuable things."

She cocked her head to one side.

"There's nothing in life that's more valuable than love and family and friendship." He kissed the back of her hand. "I've found all of those here with you."

Chapter Eighteen

"I can't believe how much we've set up in just three days," said Ivan.

Seymour looked around the office. "We had a bit of luck finding this place, but other than that, it's all been hard work and determination. You've busted your ass on this, and I appreciate it."

Ivan grinned at him. "I have, but I still haven't accomplished as much as you have. You're a beast, Mr. D."

Seymour laughed. "Thanks, I think."

"It's a compliment. I guess there was no one to talk to you like that in your old office, but this is a whole new world for you. You're going to have to get used to me—and people like me working for you."

"Working with me, Ivan. We're in this together."

Ivan nodded. "Yeah, we are. I can really feel that. You're not the kind of boss I thought you were going to be. You're right in here getting your hands dirty."

Seymour looked down at his hands.

"Literally as well as figuratively. I thought you'd stop by sometime and give orders. I didn't expect you to help clean the place and get it ready with me."

"You'll get used to the way I work."

"I thought I was." Ivan winked at him. "But now I'm not just the help, am I?"

Seymour narrowed his eyes at him. "I've said I'm sorry."

"And you don't need to. I'm just glad you met Miss Chris and woke up."

"I am, too." Seymour checked his watch. He wanted to get home to Chris soon. He'd been busy getting the office set up all week, and she'd been busy at the center.

"How many people do you think we're going to need in here? You know I'm just going along blindly so far, accepting your faith in me at face value, but I don't really get what I'm going to be doing."

Seymour smiled. "We're going to start with three people. You're going to help me hire them. We need a receptionist who'll also be your main admin person, an accountant—"

"An accountant?"

"Yes. The whole point of the office is to manage the money that comes in and make sure that it's distributed as it should be—as the donors intended."

Ivan frowned.

"What?"

"I've heard lots of times that it's not worth giving money to charities because most of the money doesn't get to where it's supposed to. It ends up paying salaries," he looked around, "and rent, and that only about twenty cents in every dollar actually goes to doing any good."

Seymour loosened his collar and sat down on the desk. "And, in general, that's true. Hopefully, it's more than twenty percent of donations, but yes, many charities are inefficient at best. We don't work that way, though."

"We don't?"

"No." Seymour didn't like to broadcast what he did, but Ivan needed to know. "I don't shout about this, but the information is available for anyone who chooses to do their due diligence before they donate. In our case, one hundred percent of donations go to the causes they're intended for."

"How? How does all of this … Oh." He looked at Seymour. "You?"

"Yes. And Clay and Oscar. We all know how fortunate we are. We've all made more money than anyone could ever need. We decided to use some of it to help people whose needs are greater than ours. We meet all the overheads so that all the donations we receive go directly to where they're needed."

"Wow."

Seymour shrugged. "It's only logical."

Ivan laughed. "It is. But most people don't use logic when it comes to money. I didn't know that about you."

"Very few people do."

"I feel bad that I assumed all your charity work was about getting tax write-offs somehow."

Seymour chuckled. "Don't feel so bad about that. Some of it is deductible. It's not that I mind paying taxes, it's just what they go to pay for that I don't always agree with. This way I get to decide how the money's spent, and I can know that it's doing more good than harm."

"That's awesome."

"It works out." Seymour's phone rang, and he pulled it out of his pocket, hoping that it was Chris. It wasn't. It was his brother, Johnny. He looked at Ivan. "Are you okay to close up? I need to take this, and then I'm going to head home."

Ivan nodded. "Sure. Have a great evening, Mr. D."

Seymour smiled at him on his way to the door. "Johnny."

"Seymour. How are you?"

"I'm doing well. How are you? How's Jean?"

"We're doing great. We're leaving Oregon tonight, heading back to the Valley. Are you there?"

"No."

"Are you in Summer Lake?"

"Yes."

He could hear the smile in his brother's voice. "That's good. And you haven't been back to the office?"

"I haven't. In fact, I'm in the process of opening a new one here."

"In Summer Lake? How's that going to work?"

"I don't mean an investment office. I'm going to be putting my time into the charity work from now on."

"That's wonderful. And am I right in thinking that you're going to be spending more time with Chris, too?"

"I'm not sticking around here for the scenery."

Johnny laughed. "I didn't think so. I'm just surprised. Happy, but surprised. Do you think you'll bring her up here so we can meet her?"

Seymour sucked in a deep breath. "I don't know. She has a full life here."

"I didn't ask if you were going to move her here, just if she might come visit. Or are you not there yet?"

"I don't know."

"Then ignore me. I know that's a tough one, and I'm not trying to push you on it. We're looking forward to meeting her, that's all."

"Are you coming to the dinner next weekend?"

"Oh, that's right. We are. I'd forgotten. Jean takes care of the schedule."

"You'll meet her then."

"Great. I'll tell Jean. Maybe get a bit of peace about it. She sends her love."

Seymour smiled to himself. He knew his sister-in-law would be thrilled with the changes that were happening in his life—happening to him. "Tell her I sent her a big hug back."

"A what?" Johnny asked, incredulously.

"You heard me. Tell her I sent her a big hug. That'll blow her mind and give her the idea of just how much I'm changing."

Johnny laughed. "If I tell her that I won't get any peace at all until I bring her to see you."

"True. Tell her I said hello then, and I'll see you both in LA next weekend."

~ ~ ~

By the time Friday rolled around, Chris was excited to go back to Malibu. She and Seymour had settled into an easy routine at the lake. They spent their evenings eating dinner out on the back patio and talking. They talked about their day and about their lives. She was loving it. She'd had some reservations about Seymour coming to stay with her on what felt like a more permanent basis, but so far things were going wonderfully.

The plan had been for them to fly to LA on Saturday with Marianne and Clay, but Seymour had suggested that they should go this afternoon. There was no reason not to, so she'd agreed.

Jeff greeted them with a smile when they got to the airport. "We're filed and ready to take off whenever you want," he said.

Seymour looked at Chris. "Are we good to go?"

"We are." It made her smile that he only let Jeff take her bag while he carried his own out to the plane.

She watched out the window as they took off, and the mountains and lake grew smaller as they climbed into the sky.

"Are you looking forward to this weekend?"

"I am. I'm looking forward to meeting Johnny and Jean. And don't worry, if you need to work tomorrow, I'm happy to hang out by the pool."

He smiled. "What makes you think I need to work?"

"I guessed that was why you wanted to go today instead of tomorrow."

"No. Do you want to know the real reason?"

"What?"

"I wanted you all to myself. I enjoy Marianne and Clay's company, but I wanted us to have this evening and tomorrow—to have dinner looking at the ocean, and to hang out by the pool or go shopping or whatever you'd like to do."

"Aww. Thank you. That's so sweet of you."

He shrugged. "I've spent a lot of time getting the office set up this week. I don't want you to think that I'm hiding in my work again. I'm not. I'm enjoying it, but part of that enjoyment comes from the fact that it allows me to be where I want to be—which is with you."

"I had wondered. I'm not complaining; I love that you're going to spend more time on the charity work, but I didn't know if it was just going to be your new addiction."

"It isn't. I don't need one anymore. I've done the work I need to do to be able to face myself and my life. My life is good, especially now that you're in it. And I'm okay with me." He smiled. "I'm not all that bad. Working with Ivan like this is showing me that. He respects me; he looks up to me."

She smiled. "I told you he did."

"I know, but I had it wrong. I thought he only looked up to me because I was able to make so much money. I didn't think it was about who I am as a person."

"I don't think money matters much to Ivan. I think that was your idea, not his."

"You're probably right. It's hard to see what you're doing when you're doing it, but I'm not anymore, and I understand now."

She laughed. "I'm glad you understand, but I don't. Can you run that one by me again and explain this time?"

"Sorry. I mean, I set myself a goal a long time ago, to make a lot of money. I met that goal but never stopped to see if I needed a new one. I just kept going after more, because that was what I did. It was what I knew. I didn't need more money. I needed to be busy and to feel like I was achieving. I forgot that other things in life were more important—and I forgot that other people didn't see money or the ability to make it in the same way I did."

"And now you get it?"

"I do. I don't need to make another penny in my life if I don't want to. I can spend as much as I want and not make a dent." He shrugged. "And I don't need to hide anymore, from anything."

"I was wondering about that. How do you feel about seeing your brother?"

"I'm looking forward to it. I'm looking forward to introducing you to him and to Jean."

"I know, but I mean, all the things you were hiding from— the main thing. You didn't want to be around Johnny and Jean because they had what you lost." She wondered whether this was a good idea now that she'd started it, but she wanted to know. "You threw yourself into your work so that you didn't have to face your life without Kate. You don't just wake up one day and decide you're over that."

His chin jerked up, and he met her gaze.

The silence drew out so long, she wondered if he was going to answer.

Eventually, he nodded. "I won't ever get over that. I loved her so much. She was a wonderful person. It broke my heart to lose her. I'll always love her." He reached across and took hold of Chris's hand. "But avoiding my family, throwing myself into work, focusing on making money, I understand now what it was all about."

She waited.

"You told me I was escaping from reality. I was. I was escaping from my own life because I didn't want a life without her in it."

She squeezed his hand, wishing she could say something that could ease the pain of loss. She knew she couldn't.

"I've lived without her for twenty years. I've had a life all that time. It's just that I didn't want to be in my life. Now I do. I want to live my life with you. You've shown me what's important. Love, family, friends. I want to be present to enjoy them. And I want to share my life with you."

Tears pricked behind Chris's eyes. "I want to share mine with you, too."

"You do?"

"Of course I do."

"I wasn't sure. I know you want me in your life, but that's different from sharing it. Don't you think?"

She cocked her head to one side.

"Maybe I'm too old school, but to me, when a man and a woman share their life, there's a word for it."

"What's the word?"

He smiled. "Marriage."

"Oh!" Her heart raced. She loved him, she believed that he loved her, but she didn't think that necessarily led to marriage. Not at their age.

His eyes were that deep green as he looked into hers. "I don't know if you feel the same way. I didn't want to spring it on you out of the blue. That's why I'm telling you how I feel now, to give you time to consider whether that's what you want."

She nodded. She didn't know what to say. To her mind, they were setting things up in an ideal way. He still got to live his life; she still got to live hers. She didn't associate being married with that kind of freedom—or understanding.

There was a touch of sadness in his eyes. "It's not something you'd consider?"

She leaned forward in her seat and cupped his cheek in her hand. "I'd like to. I need some time to think about it. What we've been talking about up until now doesn't sound like marriage to me."

"It doesn't?"

"No. We were talking about more freedom and more independence."

He smiled. "You don't think you can have those in a marriage?"

"Not in my experience."

"Isn't that what we're doing here, though? Creating a new experience. Reframing things to be how we want them to be, instead of what we thought they were supposed to be."

She nodded slowly. "I guess."

He leaned closer and kissed her. "Take your time. If it's not what you want, I'll understand. I'll be with you on any terms you want me. But I need you to know, you have my heart, you have my mind—married or not. Maybe it is just that old-school part of me, but marriage means something. It's not about obligation or owning each other. It's about committing to being a partnership."

Chris turned to look out the window again. She should be over the moon. Part of her was. Part of her was cautious—scared of something, but of what, she didn't know.

When they got to the house, Seymour parked the car in the garage and looked over at Chris. He wondered if he'd blown it, bringing up the possibility of them getting married. He knew she valued her independence. He didn't want to take that away from her. He didn't want to lose his own, but to him, marriage wasn't about giving anything up. It was about solidifying what you had.

He got out of the car, and she met him at the trunk.

"Is it strange for you to have to get your own bag?"

He smiled. "I was used to having someone to do it for me. But I don't need it. I don't miss it. It was part of that life that I don't want anymore."

She smiled back at him. "You really don't want it, do you?"

"No. I fell into it because it was what people do." He shrugged. "I'm not going to apologize for it."

Her eyes widened. "I wasn't asking you to. There's nothing wrong with it. I'm not judging."

He put his arm around her shoulders and dropped a kiss on her forehead. "I know. I think we both need to relax. I feel like I screwed things up with what I talked about earlier. I didn't mean to. I'm sorry. Can we just enjoy our time here? I wanted it to be like a little vacation with just the two of us."

She smiled. "Let's do that. I'm sorry. Come on." She took her bag from him and headed to the door that led into the kitchen. "I have my swimsuit in here, and I'm going to go put it on and then go wait for you to bring me a cocktail at the pool."

He smiled to himself as he let them in, and she trotted up the stairs to go change. That was one of the many things he loved about her. She was so willing to drop anything negative and move past it to find something good.

Chapter Nineteen

Chris looked around in awe as she stepped out of the limo. This was like one of those movie premieres—complete with red carpet and everything.

Seymour came around and took her arm. "Are you okay?"

"I am. I didn't know it was going to be like this."

He chuckled. "I did warn you to wear your best frock."

She laughed. "I know, and I was worried that I might be overdressed." She looked at the people milling around them. The men were all dressed in tuxes, the women wore evening gowns and diamonds. She turned back to Seymour. "If just a few of them donated their necklaces, you could end poverty."

He laughed out loud at that. "You're right. I've never understood why people spend so much to attend these charity dinners. I mean, the proceeds from the ticket sales are one thing, but the clothes and the limos."

Chris nodded. "You should organize one where everyone has to come in jeans and walk, bike, or drive themselves to get there—and then they can donate all the money they didn't spend on those things."

He put his arm around her shoulders and hugged her into his side. "You're a genius, Chris. That's exactly what we should do. It'd bring in so much more than this kind of event does."

She shrugged. "I'm not a genius. Anyone with a drop of common sense could have told you that."

He met her gaze, and she laughed. "I'm not telling you that you don't have any common sense."

He smiled through pursed lips. "Just that, like the people here tonight, I have more money than sense?"

She shook her head and made big innocent eyes at him. "I didn't say that."

He laughed. "Not in so many words, but you're right. I need you to keep me straight."

"Seymour!"

They'd made their way up the stairs to the entrance now. Just inside, a man was waving at them. He had to be Seymour's brother; he looked just like him.

"Are you ready to meet Johnny and Jean?"

She nodded. She was, but she was less excited than she had been. If they were the kind of people who came to events like this, she was starting to wonder how much she'd have to talk to them about. It was one thing to tease Seymour about having more money than sense—

"Chris!"

As they walked through the doors, the woman sprang forward to greet her.

Chris smiled. "You must be Jean?"

The woman nodded. "I've been dying to meet you. Do you want to get a drink? We can meet these guys at the table."

"Hey!" Her husband gave Jean a mock frown before turning to Chris. "I've been looking forward to meeting you, too." He held his hand out. "It's an honor and a pleasure. I'm Johnny."

Chris liked him immediately as she shook with him. He had a warm smile and a twinkle in his eyes.

"It's lovely to meet you."

He winked at her. "We'll talk at the table later. We'll be sitting with you. I only come to these godawful things if Seymour sits with us. That way we get to catch up with him and don't have to make small talk with all of them."

Chris had to laugh at the face he made as he gestured at the milling crowd of beautiful people.

Jean slipped her arm through Chris's. "Come on. We can get a drink at the quiet bar at the back."

Chris shot a look at Seymour, wondering how he felt about her leaving him the moment they arrived.

He took her by surprise when he cupped her cheek in his hand a landed a kiss on her lips. "Don't worry; Jean will take good care of you, and look at her—not a diamond in sight."

Chris laughed and looked at Jean. He was right. she wore no diamonds, but she was wearing a shocked expression. It matched her husband's as they both stared at Seymour. Chris guessed that they were even more surprised by his public display of affection than she'd been.

Jean tugged at her arm, and they walked away into the crowd. Chris looked back and smiled when she saw Seymour and Johnny watching them. Seymour held her gaze for a moment, and then Johnny said something to him. He answered, without looking away from her.

"He's a good man." Jean's words brought her back. She shot Seymour one last smile before they disappeared in the crowd, then turned to Jean.

"He's the best man I've ever known."

Jean smiled. "He's not perfect."

That made Chris laugh. "Who is? I know I'm not."

"And neither am I. I'm not trying to put you off. I was just testing to see if you know what you're letting yourself in for."

"I know enough."

"That's good. He really is a good man. He's been lost for a long time. Maybe you can help him find himself."

"I think what we're doing is walking beside each other while we find ourselves."

"Oh. You're a wise one. I like you already. We're going to get along just fine."

Chris smiled. She already liked Jean, too.

They took a seat at the quiet bar away from the main dining room where all the tables were set up.

Chris took a sip of her drink and looked at Jean. "So, is this kind of thing normal for you?"

Jean made a face. "You mean getting dressed up and spending the evening with a bunch of people who are mostly here to see and be seen? Who donate because it's good for their image and good for their tax return?" She let out a little laugh. "It's more normal than I'd like. Seymour does this one every year, and there are a couple of others that we're involved with, so we have to show our faces."

Chris liked her even more.

"Honestly, I'd rather be at home in Montana, making my own soup and sitting in front of the fire reading."

"That sounds more like my idea of fun."

"You should come up there. It's beautiful."

"I'd like to see Montana, but I think it'll be a while before Seymour invites me—if he ever does."

Jean nodded sadly. "I realized that as soon as I said it. I have high hopes. You're the first woman he's introduced me to in all these years. I mean, he's brought dates to these things but never someone he was seeing."

"Oh."

"He's serious about you. Johnny knew it when they talked on the phone—and if there was any doubt that he wanted the world to know about the two of you, it went up in smoke when he kissed you back there."

"He surprised me with that. He's normally more reserved in public."

Jean laughed. "But not in private?"

Chris tried not to look embarrassed, but she couldn't help laughing.

"I'm sorry. You'll get used to me. I don't know how to be fake and polite. I'd rather laugh and be real."

Chris grinned at her. "Then we're going to get along great."

"It's a good thing," said Jean, "since I get the feeling that we're going to know each other for the rest of our lives."

Chris liked the idea of that, but she didn't know what to say.

~ ~ ~

Seymour and Johnny made their way through the crowd, stopping here and there to greet people. When they finally reached the table, Johnny swiped two glasses from a tray a waiter brought by.

Seymour took one and raised it to his brother. "Here's to getting this out of the way for another year."

Johnny laughed. "Anyone would think you didn't enjoy it."

"They'd be right. I've told Clay and Oscar many a time; they're the main attraction. I'd rather stay in the background and work the numbers."

Johnny gave him a stern look. "You're just as much of an attraction as they are. And I don't just mean in terms of putting your name on it. You know as well as I do that women are the biggest donors. They enjoy coming and flirting with Clay and Oscar—but you have just as much of a draw—if not more so. Although, I'm sure there are going to be lots of disappointed ladies here this evening. Was that kiss you gave Chris for her benefit or everyone else's?"

Seymour smiled. "Honestly? It was for my benefit. She just ..." He shrugged and gave his brother a rueful smile. "She brings it out of me. I don't want to hold back, and I don't care who's watching. I'm tired of the way I've been living life—or more honestly, not living it."

Johnny nodded. "I didn't know if you'd ever get there."

"I didn't think I would, but being with Chris has changed everything. I'm tired of hiding from life. Now, I want to make the most of every moment and experience the joy of being alive."

"And you think living in that small town with her is the way to do that?"

Seymour nodded adamantly. "I do. I know it is. The only other place I'd want to be is in the valley—close to Hope and to you guys. But ..."

"But you don't know how you'll feel if you take her to the house?"

"Yes. It took me until a couple of years ago before I could face being there myself. That house was so full of Kate, so full of love. I don't know."

"Is it something you need to know? Does it matter? If you're going to live in Summer Lake with Chris ..."

"I'm going to come back to Montana often. I love spending time with Hope."

"You'll figure it out. I'm sure."

"Seymour!"

He turned as someone grasped his shoulder. It was Edward Craven, a fellow fund manager.

"Edward."

"I couldn't believe the news when I heard it. You're really putting Alan at the helm?"

"I am." He and Edward weren't exactly friends. The man was an arrogant asshole, as far as Seymour was concerned. They moved in the same circles—it was a hazard of their occupation. They courted the big investors, some went with Edward, some came to Seymour. Or now, they would come to Alan. Hopefully.

"What happened? Did the stress and pressure finally get to you? Not everyone can last forever in the high stakes games."

Seymour laughed. "No. I finally realized that the stakes just weren't high enough to warrant the stress."

Edward raised an eyebrow. "Not high enough?"

He, no doubt, thought that Seymour had found some new higher-value market to get involved in. He had. But it wasn't the kind Edward was thinking about.

"No. No matter what return the fund makes, it could never compare to the value that I've found."

"At least, give me a clue? You're killing me here. I admit it, you've hooked me. Now reel me in."

Seymour smiled. "I've discovered the simple pleasures in life, Edward—the things that are truly valuable. Love, family, community."

Edward frowned. "You're shitting me!"

Seymour and Johnny both laughed at the look on his face. "I knew you wouldn't understand. I am completely serious. You win. You can take the title of best fund manager. You beat me, you outstayed me. The glory is all yours. And you can keep it. I found a life worth so much more."

Edward walked away, shaking his head.

"He thinks you've lost it," said Johnny.

Seymour looked up and smiled when he spotted Chris and Jean coming toward the table. "I've not lost it. I've finally found it."

~ ~ ~

Chris enjoyed the evening. Johnny and Jean were great company. The four of them laughed and joked the whole time. Marianne came to join them when Clay went up on stage to sing, and she hit it off with Jean straight away, too.

When Clay came to join them, he smiled around at everyone and raised his glass. "We've been doing this dinner for a few years now, but I have to say, tonight is my favorite." He leaned over and kissed Marianne's cheek. "I never thought I'd be here with a lady of my own—let alone just a few weeks before our wedding. And you." He pointed his glass at Seymour. "I thought you were even more of a lost cause than I was." He smiled at Chris. "I've seen him smile more tonight than I'd ever seen him smile before he met you."

Seymour put his arm around her shoulders. "It's true. I thought I'd had my turn at happiness. I didn't believe I'd get another chance."

"I always hoped you would," said Jean. She smiled at Chris. "I knew it would take a special lady. And here you are."

Chris looked around the table. "I thought I was happy. I lead a full life. I have my kids and my grandkids." She smiled at Seymour. "I had no idea how much happier I could be."

"Aww. I'd guess that we'll be receiving another wedding invitation before too long," said Jean.

Seymour's arm tightened around her shoulders. She felt bad for him. She'd made clear to him that she wasn't sure that was what she wanted, and now he was being put on the spot— something she knew he didn't like.

Before she could say something that would diffuse the moment, Clay nodded at them. "That's right. And you know once we each marry a Benson sister, every one of us sitting at this table will all be family."

Chris cocked her head to one side. It was true. They'd all be brothers and sisters-in-law in some way. That gave her the warm and fuzzies.

Marianne gave her a worried look. She knew that marriage wasn't necessarily high on her priority list. Chris wanted to reassure her that it was okay, but more than that, she wanted to reassure Seymour.

She smiled at Clay. "I get you as a brother-in-law soon, anyway, but you're right." She looked at Jean and Johnny. "It'd be nice to be able to call these two family, too."

She felt Seymour tense beside her and looked up at him. He questioned her with his eyes but didn't speak. She nodded. It really wasn't such a terrible idea.

The rest of the evening went by in a blur. She chatted with what seemed like hundreds of people. Many of the women seemed less than friendly, but she didn't care. She wasn't here to get to know them. She was here to get to know Seymour better, and watching him in this environment, she did. He was more like the man she'd seen on TV. He was charming, outgoing, and now that she knew him better, she could tell he really didn't want to be there.

She got up from the table, and when he rose, she caught hold of his hand. It was fun spending time with the others, but she wanted him to herself for a while. They walked through the hotel and out into the cool night air on the terrace bar.

She leaned on the stone balustrade and he leaned beside her, looking out at the pool and the waterfall.

"Are you enjoying yourself?" he asked.

"I'd guess more than you are."

He laughed. "And I thought I hid it so well."

"You do, but not from me."

He put his arm around her. "Are you claiming that you know me better than anyone else does?"

She nodded seriously. "I am, maybe better even than you know yourself."

He met her gaze. "Maybe you do. I've managed to avoid myself for long enough."

"I wish you wouldn't do that anymore."

"I don't have to now. I like the man I'm becoming. And I love you for making me want to be him."

"I love you, Seymour."

He stood up straight and drew her to him, closing his arms around her waist and holding her against him so he could look down into her eyes. "And I love you, Chris. I'm sorry about the way conversation turned earlier. I don't want you to feel any kind of pressure."

She knew what he meant, but she wanted to make him talk about it. "What kind of pressure?"

"You know. When they talked about all of us being related."

"When they talked about us getting married?"

He nodded, looking wary. "That's what I don't want you to feel pressured about. I hope maybe someday you'll want to. But I understand if you don't. I've already told you. I want to be with you in whatever way suits you."

She smiled and reached up to plant a kiss on his lips. "But it's important to you, isn't it?"

"You know it is, but I can learn to see it differently if that's what you want."

"But in your mind, marriage is two people committing to be a team?"

He nodded.

"I think we make a pretty good team."

His lips quirked up in that cocky little smile. "I know we do. We're like two pillars standing side by side. Two strong individuals that can work together as partners—not mesh into one indistinct mess that's only known as a couple."

She laughed. "That's it. That's what I don't want to be. I don't want to lose me. I don't want you to lose you."

"And we wouldn't have to. That's not what I want from you, Chris. I want you as you are. I don't want to dilute you."

"You won't be able to."

He smiled. "I know."

She waited, wondering if he understood what she meant.

"Wait. Do you say I wouldn't be able to or won't?"

"Won't."

"Does that mean that you're open to the idea? That I *won't* be able to dilute you when we are married?"

She smiled and shrugged. "I'm not going to ask you to ask me."

He nodded and hugged her tighter. "But I am going to take my chances."

Chapter Twenty

Seymour looked up from his computer when Ivan tapped on his office door. "Come on in; what's up?"

"You have a visitor."

Seymour frowned. "Who?" He wasn't expecting anyone. Hope and Chance were coming into town this evening, but ...

"It's Hope."

"Send her in." He checked his watch, afraid that he must be falling back into his old ways and that he might have worked through the whole afternoon without noticing the time go by. But no. It was only two-thirty.

Hope peeked her head around the door. "Are you disturbable?"

He chuckled and got to his feet. "Always, for you. Come on in."

She came to him and gave him a hug. "You really have changed, haven't you?"

"Yes."

She gave him another squeeze before stepping back. "I remember when I wouldn't have dared come to your office at anything other than the appointed time."

"I'm sorry, Hopey. Those days are behind us. I want to make it up to you."

She smiled. "You don't need to. Seeing you happy is all I want. It's all I ever wanted. Well, that and having you in my life. Now I get all of that." Her smile faded. "Don't I?"

"Of course, you do. Why would you even ask?"

"Because you're living here now. And I love that for you. My only concern is how much time you'll spend up in Montana with us in the future."

"As much as I can."

"But how much can you?"

He knew what she meant. It had taken many years before he'd been able to make himself stay at the house that he and Kate had built in Paradise Valley. Since Hope had moved back up there, he'd gotten over it, but she wanted to know, and he wasn't sure how he felt about taking Chris up there.

"I think it'll be fine. We should come one of these weekends and see. I think it's just the thought of it. Once we get there, it'll be okay. You know what Chris is like. She fills every place she goes with life and laughter. I'll always miss your mom, but …"

"Don't look like that, Dad. That's what I wanted to tell you. I've been thinking about you a lot—worrying about how you'd deal with being happy again. I know how you are, and I want you to know that it's okay to be happy."

He nodded, wishing he could have back all the years he'd wasted with this wonderful daughter of his.

"I remember that Mom always used to tell me that you guys named me Hope because that was what I represented for you. That hope is what makes life worth living, and that even in the dark times, we should hold onto hope. That you guys wanted a bright future, and I was part of that."

Seymour swallowed—hard. He remembered all too well all the reasons Kate had given him for the name she wanted to give their daughter. He nodded. Not trusting himself to speak.

Hope's eyes shone with tears. "Well, I think I inherited some of Mom's wisdom, and I wanted to get you by yourself to tell you. She'd want you to have a bright future still. She'd want you to have new hope and new happiness. I do, too."

He held his arms out to her, and she flung herself into them, hugging him tightly. "I hope you'll bring Chris up there. I want you both to be part of our lives. But until you're ready, Chance and I will spend more time here. I don't want you to miss out on Dylan—and I don't want to miss out on you." She stood back and smiled at him. "Especially not on this new, chill, laid-back version of you."

He chuckled at that. "You like it?"

"I do. I mean, look at you. You're in the office, in jeans. The office is bright and casual. You're relaxed. I love it."

"I do, too." He took a deep breath and blew it out slowly. "I appreciate your support, I really do. There's something I need to tell you. I hope you're going to be happy about it."

Hope grinned. "Are you guys getting married?"

He laughed. "So much for my big surprise. I haven't asked her yet, but I think there's a good chance she'll say yes."

Hope clasped her hands together and bounced up and down on her toes. "I'm not just happy about it. I'm thrilled! She'll say yes. I know she will."

Seymour nodded. He hadn't known how long it would take for Chris to be open to the idea of getting married. She'd surprised him at the fundraiser dinner when she'd told him, in a roundabout way, that she was. He'd second guessed himself in the weeks since and had checked with her in every way he could think—without coming out and asking her—that it really was what she wanted. She'd reassured him each time. When they'd been at dinner with her boys the other night, she'd even dropped a hint about getting impatient.

"I hope so because I don't want to wait any longer. I hope you and Chance are going to come over to the house tomorrow evening."

Hope's eyes widened. "Are you going to …?"

He nodded.

"We wouldn't miss it."

~ ~ ~

Chris looked around and smiled. The bar was busier than usual this afternoon. She waved at Abbie, who was sitting at a corner booth with Michael's wife, Megan. They'd offered her the job as his new receptionist, and Chris guessed that Abbie and Megan would become friends. Although she'd wanted Abbie to leave town and go and make a new life for herself somewhere else, she was starting to see things differently after their last conversation. Abbie had made her realize that just as parents wanted the best for their grown children, their children wanted the best for them, too.

Hers certainly did. She knew that much. She smiled when she saw Jack and Dan come in through the doors side by side. She was so proud of them. They were such good-looking men, if she did say so herself. They were different in many ways— Jack was the outgoing one; Dan was quieter. Jack brought people together. Dan preferred his own company. But they both spread goodness in the world. They'd both found their perfect partner and were getting on with building their lives.

"Hey, Mom." Dan leaned in to kiss her cheek.

Jack did the same. When he straightened up, he gave her a stern look. "We deliberately came early so that you wouldn't sit around at the bar by yourself. You know my thoughts on you doing that."

She laughed. "You can think whatever you like. I'm not going to stop it. I told Seymour the same thing."

Jack chuckled. "And he has to accept it. I know you won't take it from him. I know you won't listen to me either, but I'm not going to stop telling you."

She shrugged. "You do what you need to, but I will, too."

Dan shook his head. "You two will never change, will you?"

"If you mean I'll never meekly do as my son tells me, then no."

Jack laughed. "And if you mean will I give up on looking out for Mom, then that's a no from me, too."

"At least, I got you both to agree on something."

"Are we going to get a table?" asked Jack.

Once they were seated in one of the booths, Chris looked at them both. "So, what's going on with you?"

"Business as usual," said Jack. "We're getting ready to start on Phase Three over at Four Mile Creek." He raised an eyebrow at her. "There are going to be some custom homes up on the ridge if you're interested."

"Why would I be interested? I love my house."

"What about Seymour?"

"He loves my house, too."

"Does he really?" asked Dan.

"Yes, he does. Don't you two go thinking that things are going to change now that he's living with me. He's enjoying my place. He has other big fancy houses he can visit whenever he wants."

Dan nodded. "As long as you're happy."

"I am. We are. I don't plan on making any big changes."

Jack and Dan exchanged a look she didn't understand.

"What?" she asked. "If you've got something to say, then say it."

The server came to take their order, and once she'd gone, Jack met Chris's gaze.

"I guess all I really want to say is that if you do want to make any changes, we're on board with it."

She frowned. "What are you talking about?"

"Nothing." Dan shot a look at Jack.

She knew there was something going on with them, but she didn't know what. "Would one of you please tell me?"

"There's nothing to tell," said Dan. "We just want you to know that we're happy for you."

"That's right."

She shook her head. "Thank you. But that doesn't feel like news to me. You've both been over to the house. Seymour and I have been out with all of you. Everyone seems to get along. So, why are you making a big deal out of it all of a sudden?"

Dan smirked and jerked his head at Jack. "You know what he's like, sometimes he just gets a bee in his bonnet."

Chris laughed. "I suppose. Anyway, if we're done with that, tell me what else is going on with you both."

She enjoyed their company. It had been a while since they'd done this. The three of them came out to eat every so often. Most of the time, she saw one of them and their wives or their kids, but these dinners that they had were special.

Chris put her fork down and sat back with a smile.

"Hey, there's Laura," said Jack.

Chris turned and waved at her niece, who was standing by the bar. Laura came over and grinned at them. "What's this, a Benson family reunion? Why wasn't I invited?"

Chris smiled. "It's just the boys and me this time, but we should do it again soon with your mom and you."

"It'll have to be very soon, or we'll have to invite Clay—he'll be family, too, in a couple of weeks. And then—"

She stopped short when Jack scowled at her.

"Is everything ready for the wedding?" asked Dan.

It wasn't like him to ask about wedding plans. Chris could tell there was some undercurrent between the three of them, but she didn't know what it was about. Jack stopped scowling, and Laura started chattering on about Marianne and the wedding arrangements.

After Laura excused herself, Chris looked at the boys. "Are you sure you don't want to tell me what's going on?"

Jack shrugged, and Dan laughed. "Are you sure you don't know what's going on?"

"I have no idea."

Jack shook his head. "I wasn't sure if you were just playing along. You really don't know?"

"I don't, but one of you had better tell me."

"Sorry, no can do," said Jack.

Dan smiled at her. "Don't get frustrated. You'll know soon enough."

"Well, if it's a surprise, it'd better be a good one."

"The best," said Jack. He looked at his watch. "I should get going."

"Aren't we going to hang out for a while?"

Dan smiled at her. "We'll see you again soon. Very soon. But we need to get going. You should, too. Seymour's probably home by now."

She frowned. "So? He knows I'm having dinner with you two."

Jack smiled. "And I'm sure he's looking forward to seeing you."

Chris laughed. "You've changed your tune about him."

"I have. He's a good man. I trust him to make you happy."

"I do, too," added Dan.

"Aww, thanks, boys." Her chest filled with warmth, and her eyes pricked with tears. Maybe this was what the undercurrent had been about. They were letting her know that they approved of Seymour. "You know, I'm old enough and wise and enough to make my own decisions, but it means a lot."

Dan smiled at her. "We also know that you've always factored us into your decisions. So, when you have to make another one, we want you to know where we stand."

She cocked her head to one side. "Thank you." She didn't always understand the way he said things, but she knew it was just his way of saying he supported her.

"Come on," said Jack. "Time to go."

Chris pulled up in the driveway, still a little surprised to be home this early. She got out of the car with a smile. Maybe Seymour would want to go for a walk.

She let herself in and called for him. There was no reply.

"Seymour? Are you here?" That was strange. His car was outside. She ran upstairs to see if he was in the shower. Nope. Oh well. Hope and Chance were in town. Maybe he was with them. He wasn't expecting her home yet.

She went back down to the kitchen and poured herself a glass of wine then went to fetch her Kindle from the living room. She could sit outside and read.

When she stepped out through the patio doors, she stopped. He was standing there, smiling at her and holding a big bunch of roses. "There you are!"

"Here I am."

He came to her and took her hand, bringing her outside. "These are for you."

She set down her glass and took the flowers, bringing them up to smell them. "They're beautiful. Thank you."

"You're beautiful, Chris. And you've made my life beautiful."

"Aww." She set the flowers down on the table and slid her arms up around his neck. "I love you."

He closed his arms around her. "And I love you. There's something I want to ask you."

"What?"

He smiled. "I've imagined this moment so many different ways, but this is how it should be. Here, just you and me."

She cocked her head to one side. "What mo ... oh!"

Her hand came up to cover her mouth as he got down on one knee before her and held up a ring. "The moment where I ask you to marry me, to spend the rest of your life with me. The moment where I tell you that you've changed my life, changed me for the better and that I want to spend the rest of our days together. I love you, Chris. You've made me a better man. Say you'll marry me?"

She nodded, and he slipped the ring onto her finger.

He got to his feet and closed his arms around her. His eyes were that beautiful green as he lowered his lips to kiss her. When he did, the familiar wave of desire coursed through her, and she wanted to drag him upstairs. But when they came up for air, and she opened her eyes, she had to blink a few times. They weren't alone in her backyard anymore. The boys stood there grinning at her, their wives by their sides with their kids. Hope and Chance were there, Marianne and Clay, Laura and her husband, Smoke—even Ivan. She looked at Seymour then looked back at them.

"What? Where did you—?"

Seymour laughed and slid his arm around her shoulders. "I wasn't sure you'd say yes. I made everyone wait outside the fence in case you said no."

"We tried to tell him it'd be okay," said Jack with a smile.

Chris laughed. "How did you beat me back here?"

"We almost didn't," said Dan.

"So," realization dawned on her, "this is what the two of you meant about supporting me in any decisions I had to make?"

Jack nodded. "Yeah." He held her gaze for a moment, and she understood. They wanted her to be happy—and she was. She looked up at Seymour and landed a kiss on his lips. "Aren't you the sneaky one?"

He laughed. "I'm the lucky one."

Marianne went inside and came back out with a tray full of champagne glasses. While the boys popped and poured, she came and hugged Chris.

"Were you in on this, too?"

"Of course, I was a still a little wary, though."

Chris smiled. "I was, too, but I'm not anymore."

Marianne hugged her. "I'm so glad. I know he'll be good to you."

Chris hugged her back. "And I know I'll be good to him."

"He was right when he said he's a lucky man."

Chris laughed. "Maybe so, but I'm a lucky lady, too."

Seymour and Clay brought them each a glass of champagne, and after congratulatory hugs all around, Clay smiled at them. "I never dreamed that I'd find love this late in life."

"Me neither," said Marianne. "And it's like a dream come true that both my sister and I have found it with such wonderful guys."

Chris nodded. "Not so long ago I would have told you that falling in love again and getting married was a dream too far."

Seymour hugged her to him. "I would, too. But now we know there's no such thing."

She looked up into his eyes, and he dropped a kiss on her lips. She wanted to pinch herself to make sure she wasn't really dreaming. But his strong reassuring arm around her reminded her that this was real. This was her life, and she was eager to get on with living the rest of it, with him by her side;

;

A Note from SJ

I hope you enjoyed Seymour and Chris's story. Please let your friends know about the books if you feel they would enjoy them as well. It would be wonderful if you would leave me a review, I'd very much appreciate it.

Check out the "Also By" page to see if any of my other series appeal to you – I have a couple of ebook freebie series starters, too, so you can take them for a test drive.

There are a few options to keep up with me and my imaginary friends:

The best way is to Sign up for my Newsletter at my website www.SJMcCoy.com. Don't worry I won't bombard you! I'll let you know about upcoming releases, share a sneak peek or two and keep you in the loop for a couple of fun giveaways I have coming up :0)

You can join my readers group to chat about the books or like my Facebook Page www.facebook.com/authorsjmccoy
I occasionally attempt to say something in 140 characters or less(!) on Twitter

And I'm in the process of building a shiny new website at www.SJMcCoy.com

I love to hear from readers, so feel free to email me at SJ@SJMcCoy.com if you'd like. I'm better at that! :0)

I hope our paths will cross again soon. Until then, take care, and thanks for your support—you are the reason I write!

Love

SJ

PS Project Semicolon

You may have noticed that the final sentence of the story closed with a semi-colon. It isn't a typo. <u>Project Semi Colon</u> is a non-profit movement dedicated to presenting hope and love to those who are struggling with depression, suicide, addiction and self-injury. Project Semicolon exists to encourage, love and inspire. It's a movement I support with all my heart.

"A semicolon represents a sentence the author could have ended, but chose not to. The sentence is your life and the author is you." - Project Semicolon

This author started writing after her son was killed in a car crash. At the time I wanted my own story to be over, instead I chose to honour a promise to my son to write my 'silly stories' someday. I chose to escape into my fictional world. I know for many who struggle with depression, suicide can appear to be the only escape. The semicolon has become a symbol of support, and hopefully a reminder – Your story isn't over yet

Also by SJ McCoy

Summer Lake Silver
Clay and Marianne in Like Some Old Country Song
Seymour and Chris in A Dream Too Far

Summer Lake Seasons
Angel and Luke in Take These Broken Wings
Zack and Maria in Too Much Love to Hide

Summer Lake Series
Love Like You've Never Been Hurt (FREE in ebook form)
Work Like You Don't Need the Money
Dance Like Nobody's Watching
Fly Like You've Never Been Grounded
Laugh Like You've Never Cried
Sing Like Nobody's Listening
Smile Like You Mean It
The Wedding Dance
Chasing Tomorrow
Dream Like Nothing's Impossible
Ride Like You've Never Fallen
Live Like There's No Tomorrow
The Wedding Flight

Remington Ranch Series
Mason (FREE in ebook form) and also available as Audio
Shane
Carter
Beau
Four Weddings and a Vendetta

A Chance and a Hope
Chance is a guy with a whole lot of story to tell. He's part of the fabric of both Summer Lake and Remington Ranch. He needed three whole books to tell his own story.

Chance Encounter
Finding Hope
Give Hope a Chance

Love in Nashville
Autumn and Matt in Bring on the Night

The Davenports
Oscar
TJ
Reid

The Hamiltons
Cameron and Piper in Red wine and Roses
Chelsea and Grant in Champagne and Daisies
Mary Ellen and Antonio in Marsala and Magnolias
Marcos and Molly in Prosecco and Peonies
Coming Next
Grady

About the Author

I'm SJ, a coffee addict, lover of chocolate and drinker of good red wines. I'm a lost soul and a hopeless romantic. Reading and writing are necessary parts of who I am. Though perhaps not as necessary as coffee! I can drink coffee without writing, but I can't write without coffee.

I grew up loving romance novels, my first boyfriends were book boyfriends, but life intervened, as it tends to do, and I wandered down the paths of non-fiction for many years. My life changed completely a few years ago and I returned to Romance to find my escape.

I write 'Sweet n Steamy' stories because to me there is enough angst and darkness in real life. My favorite romances are happy escapes with a focus on fun, friendships and happily-ever-afters, just like the ones I write.

These days I live in beautiful Montana, the last best place. If I'm not reading or writing, you'll find me just down the road in the park - Yellowstone. I have deer, eagles and the occasional bear for company, and I like it that way :0)